T0370418

THE CASE OF THE RUSSIAN DOLL

BY

ERICA AXELROD

authorHOUSE

AuthorHouse™
1663 Liberty Drive
Bloomington, IN 47403
www.authorhouse.com
Phone: 833-262-8899

This is a work of fiction. All of the characters, names, incidents,
organizations, and dialogue in this novel are either the products
of the author's imagination or are used fictitiously.

Published by AuthorHouse 05/01/2024

ISBN: 979-8-8230-2554-6 (sc)
ISBN: 979-8-8230-2553-9 (e)

Library of Congress Control Number: 2024908073

Print information available on the last page.

Any people depicted in stock imagery provided by Getty Images are
models, and such images are being used for illustrative purposes only.
Certain stock imagery © Getty Images.

This book is printed on acid-free paper.

A Note to the Reader:

Over the past decade, much has changed in the political climate of Haiti. However, this work of fiction represents the pursuit of freedom for all immigrants who have risked their lives to be a part of this great nation.

Erica Axelrod

To Jefferson, my parents, and my children with love.

CHAPTER 1

Haitian soldiers in yellow uniform burst through
the door and charged through the house with their
machetes, slashing through furniture and knocking
over lamps and glass. Nina guided Amandine to the
back of the house, pushed out a window with her bare
hand and boosted her friend through the hole amidst
jagged glass. Behind them, she could hear the clamor
of their boots moving closer. Nina mounted up to the
window with her own strength, straddled her legs over
the ledge and landed with her feet in the sand.

They held hands, dashing along the beach, pebbles
cutting into Nina's skin underneath the thong of her
sandal. Her other hand was bleeding badly from the
slivers of glass. Amandine tore off some fabric from
the bottom of her sundress and used it as a tourniquet

for Nina's wound. Then she doubled over to try to catch her breath.

Nina could hear them in the distance, shouting in Creole. Alongside her was the sea, innocent and serene. "Come on. We need to keep running."

"I can't make it." Amandine was wheezing.

Nina embraced her with a firm grip on the crux of her arm, pulling her along, and as if transcended out of time and place with super strength and speed, they made their way to a wooden cottage by the shore.

Theron, the fisherman, was sitting on a rocking chair on a dilapidated porch. He had weathered dark skin, a gray colored beard and smiling eyes above his pipe. Amandine spoke to him in Creole and he hid them in a secret compartment inside the cottage in the back wall. It smelled of mildew and the stale air was suffocating. They sat with their backs pressed against the door, soaking it with the perspiration from their damp dresses.

Earlier that morning, they had been carefree, lying on the beach in their bikinis in the back of Amandine's father's mansion, sipping margaritas and reading fashion magazines when Amandine's brother, Blaise, had come through the gate. He strolled up and down the beach with a tripod and camera, kneeling, snapping pictures.

Nina went to the shore and kicked a hackey sack around, then bounced it off her knee towards Blaise, but he missed it and it fell in the sea.

He scooped it out of the wet sand and returned it to Nina. She placed it on her towel to dry, then painted her toenails in black polish while Amandine did the backstroke in the sea.

"What are the pictures for?" Nina asked.

"I'm doing a documentary on Haitian culture to bring back with me to the States." He snapped one of Amandine emerging out of the water in her blue bikini. "That one's for my professor."

"Give me that." Amandine took the camera and ran with it, Blaise chasing after her.

"Hey, give it back. I need it for the meeting."

Amandine came to a halt, and pivoted to face her brother. "What meeting?"

He looked down. "I didn't want to tell you."

She lunged towards him. "Tell me. What's going on?"

"A komite katie," he spoke softly, looking around him to make sure no one was listening.

Nina covered herself with a sundress, put on sandals and followed after the pair to a small schoolhouse at a remote part of Port-Au-Prince. It had stuccoed facades in pink and a red tiled roof. Inside, benches were packed with nearly forty people, passing out literature that featured a Haitian man with glasses.

"What's going on?" Nina whispered.

"You don't know?"

Nina shook her head.

"These people want Aristide to be restored to power." She pointed to the man's face that was on buttons and T-shirts. "We used these to get him elected, but last year, a coup ousted him from power." She studied Nina's face. "You shouldn't have followed us here."

"Well, what was I supposed to do?"

"You should've stayed at the house."

When the meeting started, Amandine and Blaise were received with accolades. The leader acknowledged them, speaking in Creole between interludes of applause. The tonal sounds of voices were cohesive and passionate.

"Why are you given such attention?"

"Because my father has friends in the present government and we are deserters for their cause."

"What if you get caught?"

"We could be killed."

Nina's eyes widened in alarm.

"Don't worry. We'll be back in the States tonight."

But during the meeting, holding hands in a song of peace, soldiers came through the doors, charging down the aisle. The people recoiled in horror, shrieking as they fled through the back of the schoolhouse. Blaise led Nina and Amandine to hide behind a bookshelf, then left them to skirt around the room, snapping pictures of the scene, until he was forced to escape out the first floor window.

Nina crouched down, but managed to keep her hands on her ears to try to block out the guttural screams of the people being arrested, still she could hear them wailing for what seemed forever, and then it ended as quickly as it began into a dead calm.

When the soldiers had vanished, Nina and Amandine remained still, until Blaise returned through the front door with an armed soldier.

"Come out. It's okay."

Nina and Amandine crawled out from behind the bookshelf on their hands and knees.

Blaise gestured towards the soldier. "Alain, here, says there are soldiers all around. They are burning the propaganda. Some have machetes."

Alain helped Amandine to her feet, holding her hand, speaking in Creole.

"He says we must go away from here and never come back." Blaise translated for Nina. "They know we were here. It has been reported. They'll be looking for us."

Alain led them to their cousin's house and Blaise decided that he should gather some supplies for their journey immediately.

"But if the soldiers come for you, you must run to Theron's cottage. Do not go to the airport, Amandine. They will kill you. Give Theron this money and he will take you to the boats." He placed some money in Amandine's palm. Then he turned to Nina. "Look, you don't have to stay here. No one is looking for you." He fetched his camera and hung it around Nina's neck with the strap. "Here, take this to America."

It was shortly after that the soldiers came looking for them with their machetes, where Nina hoisted Amandine out the window, and they ran for their lives.

Erica Axelrod

CHAPTER 2

The Village Coffee Shop was down the block from Washington Square Park, adjacent to Nina's dormitory, Hayden Hall. It was a small, old-fashioned diner with several red, upholstered booths, formica tables and about eight stools lined at the counter top. The waiters looked tired and bored as they took orders from customers at the early morning hour. Not far behind the counter was the kitchen, noisy and full of bacon smoke. Sitting on a stool, Nina looked down at the menu.

The waitress wrote down her order on a pad, tore off a sheet and passed it to the line cook through the open window of the kitchen.

"Hey Randy, look who's here." Nicholas wiped his hands on his apron.

Nina sat quietly, lighting a cigarette.

6

Randy grabbed a cigarette from her pack and lit one too. "When did you get back?"

"Just now."

"How was Haiti?"

"A nightmare."

He regarded her curiously. "Why? Where's Amandine?"

"Shshsh! No names." She put her bandaged finger up to her lips.

Randy touched it. "What happened to you?"

"I'll tell you later." She talked through clamped teeth. "So what's going on here?"

"A talent agent came in here, a big one. I gave him your resume."

She feigned a smile.

"You don't seem very happy. I thought you'd be happy. I mean all you ever do is talk about agents." He disappeared for a moment, then returned with her food and sat on a stool next to her.

"I'm thankful for your efforts, but it just doesn't seem that important right now."

"I don't understand."

She looked down, poking her eggs with her fork, allowing the yellow goo to flow around the cracks in the plate, making designs.

"You seem very disturbed." He whispered. "Come with me and Nicholas for some drinks when our shift is over."

At around 4:00 a.m., the three of them climbed to the rooftop of Randy's apartment on West 14th Street.

They leaned against the wall near the edge of the roof as Randy pulled out some beer. Nina folded her arms to her chest, shivering.

Randy walked towards the door. "I'll get you a jacket."

Nicholas moved away from the wall and squatted in front of the case of beer. He picked up one, then flicked the cap towards the garbage can. It bounced off the tip of the can's mouth and fell towards the ground. "I'm losing my touch."

Nina said nothing, but picked up his cap and threw it in the garbage.

A few moments later, Randy returned with an old high school football jacket with a varsity letter falling halfway off the chest. He draped it around Nina.

"Thank you."

"Oh, it's nothing. Keep it. I haven't used this old thing in years."

Nina shuffled to the edge of the rooftop and looked around. Directly in front of her, she could see another dilapidated apartment house and down below, she saw a dark and vacant alley. She turned to look at Randy. He yawned, displaying his tobacco tinted teeth. Nina did not have any more cigarettes so she chewed on one of Nicholas' cigars.

As she sat on the wall drinking a beer, she allowed her feet to dangle over the edge. She watched two cats slink into the alley. They rummaged through the garbage for their midnight feast, looking a bit like oversized rats with long tails. The fat one, disappointed by his fare, slithered deep into the trenches of the trash.

When Nina cried softly, Randy came over to her and embraced her from behind.

"What's wrong Nin? Come on, what's going on?"

Nina caught her breath. "Okay, I'll tell you. But you have to promise you won't tell anyone."

"I promise."

She looked over at Nicholas.

"Promise." He repeated.

"Okay, I'll tell you." She cleared her throat and told them the story about what happened in Haiti.

Nicholas' eyes were wide. "So where's Amandine?"

"I don't know," she cried. "She's somewhere in the ocean on a wooden boat."

Randy pulled Nina off of the wall and held her. "What do you mean a wooden boat?"

"Well, after the soldiers left the house by the seashore, we felt safe and came out to talk to the fisherman who lived there. He gave Amandine some papers and took us to this place where people were climbing onto a wooden boat. Amandine told the fisherman to take me back to the airport because they wouldn't be looking for me. But she insisted on going on this boat that was headed for Florida."

"Why?" Randy asked.

"She said they would kill her if she stayed."

Randy's face was drawn. "That's terrible. But what will happen when she gets here?"

"If she gets here." Nicholas said.

Randy slapped him on the arm. "Let's try to be a little sensitive here."

Nina looked off in the distance. "I have no idea how long it will take her. She must be so cold." Nina shuddered. "She was only wearing a sundress. And she kept saying to me that I need to get her a lawyer."

"Why a lawyer?"

Nicholas raised his eyebrow. "You don't know?" He paused, regarding them critically. "Because they'll send her back to Haiti, that's why."

Nina got down into a squat and opened another beer. She chugged some down, then put the can between her knees and wiped her nose in an old tissue that was in the pocket of her jeans. She had changed in the bathroom of the airport. "She looked at me from the boat, and I promised her. I promised I would get her a lawyer." She nibbled at her shortened nails. "I'm going to McNamara & Associates in the morning."

"That's the biggest firm in the city. They don't do that kind of work," Nicholas said.

"They do everything if you slip them enough bucks," Randy said.

"I have some money from tips."

Nicholas narrowed his eyes. "What do you think an attorney can do for you now?"

"I'm just lining things up. I promised her that when she gets here..."

"If she gets here."

"You know, you're making this worse."

Nicholas grabbed Nina's hand. "I'm sorry. I don't mean to be insensitive, but I think you'd be wasting your time at an attorney's office."

"Why?"

"Attorneys cost a lot of money and it doesn't sound like Amandine's father will be supporting her cause."

"I promised her. She's my best friend." Her eyes were sorrowful.

"I'm sorry. I'm not trying to make you more upset."

"You have no idea what it was like. They were on this flimsy boat headed for the cold sea."

Nicholas puffed on his cigar as he looked at Randy to say something.

Randy strolled towards Nina, then put his hand on her shoulder. "Look Nin, there's no need to get mad at Nicholas. He just didn't want you to waste your time."

"It's very hard for me to believe that the two people I trusted more than anyone would be so callous." Nina raised her voice and bit down on her lip, trying not to cry again. Then she walked away, proceeding down the fire escape.

She strolled around the city, watching the sunrise. She passed the Statue of Liberty at Battery Park. There was a young, homeless mother who was sleeping on a bench next to a child. The mother did not have a blanket, but wrapped her daughter in an old, stained sheet. Nina placed Randy's football jacket across the mother and tiptoed away.

At 9:00 a.m., Nina arrived at McNamara & Associates.

"How can I help you?" The receptionist flashed a superior grin.

"Good morning. My name is Nina Pavlova. Can I have an appointment with Mr...," she looked down at the yellow pages, "Mr. Jim McNamara."

"I don't think so." The receptionist snickered. "Mr. McNamara charges five hundred dollars just to have a consultation."

Nina pounded her fist on the desk. "That's outrageous."

"Sorry." She shrugged, making a helpless gesture. "Mr. McNamara is one of the most well-known attorneys in the world."

"I need to speak to a lawyer." Nina leaned forward as if she was speaking to a confidant. "Isn't there anyone I can talk to?"

"Well, Ms. Frank will on occasion see walk-ins." She picked up the phone receiver to her ear. "Sit down. I'll see if she's available."

At 11:10 a.m., Nina was sitting in Yvonne Lindell-Frank's office and was missing her improvisation class at the university.

"Good morning," Nina said. "You have no idea how happy I am to see you."

Lindell-Frank closed the door and took a seat behind her desk. She wore a chalk-striped suit and a woman's tie.

"What can I help you with?" she asked, picking up her legal pad.

Nina relayed the entire incident as the attorney took fast notes and flipped through her pages.

"And what would you like this office to do?"

"I would like you to help Amandine become a citizen when she reaches America. She can't go back to Haiti. Her life is in danger."

Frank nodded, picked up her pad and walked into the hallway to speak to someone. Nina pushed her chair forward to try to hear their discussion, but was not close enough. It sounded like a quiet, sequence of sounds.

After about ten minutes, Lindell-Frank brought an older man with a bull neck into her office and introduced him to Nina. "Ms. Pavlova, this is the senior partner of the firm, Jim McNamara."

Nina shook his hand. "Pleased to meet you."

"Look my dear, I'm sorry to say this, but you can't conduct immigration proceedings with a missing petitioner. You've got to know for certain that she's going to arrive safely on that boat." He had a Southern drawl. "You see, I <u>think</u> the Cowboys are going to win the Super Bowl this year, but I don't know that for certain so I'm not placing any bets yet." He hooted, poking Lindell-Frank in the side.

Nina shook her head as she choked back tears.

"What you need is a live petitioner and a lot of money," Lindell-Frank said. "And even with that, it is very difficult to put on a political asylum case."

"Why?"

"Well, evidence of things that go on in Haiti is not readily available."

"I have a camera with pictures of the night we were chased by the police."

"Where is it?" Lindell-Frank suddenly looked interested.

"In Haiti," Nina said. "In a secret compartment in a cottage by the shore. I think I could remember how to get there."

McNamara gave a belly laugh. "I don't think our attorneys would be interested in poking around some cottage in Port-Au-Prince. Do you?" He asked Lindell-Frank.

"Ah, I don't think so."

"Maybe you can find some bleeding heart attorney in Miami to help you with this case, but our firm isn't interested." He walked towards the door.

"And what could this bleeding heart do?" She called after him.

"Well, he might do it for free," McNamara said. "Then you could save your money to buy some new jeans." He pointed to the large hole in her knee. "Young ladies like you shouldn't be walking around this city dressed like that."

Nina crossed her left leg in front of the hole and looked up at him. "Why is it all about money? Don't you want justice? What's wrong with you people? There's a woman who is out on a wooden boat somewhere, risking her life to be part of our country, and all you care about is money! Doesn't anyone have any compassion? What's wrong—"

"Look, I can understand that you're upset. But honey, I'm going to have to ask you to calm down." McNamara put his finger to his lips to silence her, then walked out of the room.

As Nina was about to leave, Lindell-Frank put her hand on Nina's arm. "Look, if somehow you get a hold of that camera and it's worthwhile, I might be interested in this case," she said thoughtfully.

Nina nodded and stared at the elevator as she awaited the doors to open.

Lindell-Frank stepped closer. "You know, it's hard on us too when people come in here upset that something happened to them and we can't help. I don't know, you'd have to be a lawyer to understand."

After Nina left the office, she walked aimlessly around the city. She strolled past the homeless who were begging for food. She stuffed her hands in her pocket, pulled out some coins and dropped them into their tin cups. She recognized many of them and they often waved to her when she would come by. She had lived in the city since she was six years old when her mother, Natasia, defected from Russia, fleeing from her ballerina troupe at a New York theater.

Nina remembered back to the earlier years when they lived in the back room of another family's apartment in Brooklyn. The woman made Nina stew every night and her husband would frown all the time or pick vegetables out of his teeth. Then one day, Natasia got a job dancing in the chorus line at Radio City. She made enough money for them to get their own apartment.

They moved across the street where they had their own kitchen and bathroom.

That evening, Nina walked into her dormitory, Hayden Hall. She checked her mail and messages, no calls. She climbed up the stairs to her room.

"Hello," said a girl with auburn hair, sitting on Amandine's bed.

"Who are you?"

"Remmy Peterson." She stood to her feet, extending her hand.

"Who let you in my room?"

Remmy flashed a key. "I did. I'm your new roomy."

"I don't need a new roomy. I already have one."

"Well, I don't know. I was on the waiting list for this dorm and they just informed me that there was an opening."

"Who informed you?"

"The Department of Housing." She moved towards Nina. "I'm in law school, but I wanted to dorm with the undergraduates. The grads are way too serious."

Nina stormed out of the room, slamming the door.

Remmy chased her down the hall. "Wait. Come back. Maybe we can work this out. How about some hot tea?"

Remmy poured some tea into a porcelain cup and handed it to Nina.

"Thank you," Nina said as she sniffed the fruity aroma. "So how's law school?"

"I wouldn't know. I haven't gone to a class yet."

"So why are you there?"

"My grandfather is owner of Peterson & Peterson, one of the largest firms in the city. I have no choice."

"How sad." Nina sipped the tea and grimaced at the sweet taste, then she slipped into their bathroom, pouring the rest of it down the toilet, watching it flow into the bowl. When she was little, she used to think little KGB men lived down in the bottom of the commode, plotting to come up and yank her and Natasia back to Russia.

That night, she lay in bed with the covers up to her chin. When she finally fell asleep, she dreamed that Amandine was adrift at sea, the water enveloping her and almost swallowing her into the jaws of the waves. She swam on her belly, trying to gasp for air, her body listless... and Lindell-Frank said, "You'd have to be a lawyer to understand."

"Wake up, Nina. You've been sleeping forever. You're gonna miss your class."

Nina opened her eyes. Remmy was peering down at her.

"You should talk," Nina said, turning on her side.

She heard footsteps moving away from her. "Suit yourself."

Nina faked sleep as she listened to the blow-drying and spraying of hair. She had to cover her nose and mouth with the covers because the fumes from the spray were making her gag. "I'm leaving," Remmy finally said. "I think I'll audit your improvisation class. Do you want me to tell your professor anything?"

Nina shook her head, then stuffed it under her pillow.

"Suit yourself. But you don't know how lucky you are to pursue theater."

After a few moments, Nina heard the faint sound of the door closing.

When Remmy was gone, Nina got out of bed and went down the hall to take a shower. She stood still as the hot water gushed over her body, causing her skin to turn red. She watched as the dirty water accumulated around her toes, dirt from Haitian soil safely immigrated to the States, until now. She took a bottle of soap, poured it all over her body and watched it run into the drain. She kicked at the bubbles with her feet, then crouched against the wall, sobbing into her hands as the water drizzled in her ears.

When the water turned icy, Nina jumped up and turned it off. She grabbed a towel and wrapped it tightly around herself to keep warm. When she was dry, she scurried back to her room and shut the door.

After Nina got dressed, she went outside to find the subway to Park Slope. She planned on visiting Soloman Horowitz, Natasia's attorney. He had helped them to become American citizens and had remained a close friend of the family. He was older now, and recently retired.

As Nina ambled down the sidewalks of Park Slope, she became nostalgic as she remembered being a child, skipping freely over the cracks and watching the well-dressed girls play jump rope and jacks. Nina had often wished she and Natasia could move into the brownstone that the Horowitz family lived where the house always smelled like fabulous cooking and everything was beautiful. Mr. Horowitz had always given Nina books to read, then took the time to discuss them with her. She walked up to the front door and banged on it with the brass knocker. She could hear some shuffling around until Mrs. Horowitz opened the door. She was an adorable, elderly lady who never went anywhere without wearing high heel shoes and pink lipstick.

"Well, hello! It's so good to see you." She pulled Nina close to her and kissed her on the head. "Come on in. You're going to catch a cold dressed like that." She looked at Nina's exposed navel and hip-huggers. "All grown up now. Little Nina." She waved her inside.

Nina followed her into the dining room.

"Sit down. I just made some lunch."

Nina looked at the table. It had a spread of bagels, whitefish, freshly cut vegetables and cream cheese on pretty, pastel trays.

"Sit. You need to eat. You're too thin."

Nina smiled as she sat down at the table. She spread some cream cheese and tomato on a half of a sesame bagel, then took a bite. "Oh, this is wonderful. Thank you."

"Of course." Mrs. Horowitz went into the kitchen and poured Nina a glass of orange juice. "So how's your mother?"

"She's fine." Nina answered with her mouth half full.

"Is she dancing?"

"Kind of. She's teaching ballroom dancing in a condo in Florida."

Mrs. Horowitz frowned. "She shouldn't be doing that."

"Why not?"

"She's a good dancer. She should be dancing."

"Well, she's getting older."

"Natasia?" She waved her hand in the air. "She'll never get old."

Nina gave a polite laugh and finished her bagel. "So where's Mr. Horowitz?"

"Ha. He's probably in the back room yelling at the television." She moved closer to Nina, lowering her voice. "He likes to watch court shows and yell at the lawyers. He should never have retired."

"What? You don't like me hanging around Sadie?" a male voice asked.

Nina whipped her head around and saw Mr. Horowitz standing in the doorway. His hair was all white and his eyes always danced like he was about to tell a joke. Nina ran over to him. "Mr. Horowitz. How are you?" She gave him a strong hug.

He looked at her, beaming. "What a wonderful surprise. And to what do we owe this visit?"

Nina looked down at her feet. She felt ashamed that she had not visited them since she started college.

"She must be in trouble," Mrs. Horowitz said.

"Well, nobody comes to see me unless they're in trouble." He took his finger under Nina's chin and looked into her eyes. "So what is it? What did you do?"

Nina looked over at Mrs. Horowitz who stood there with her hands on her hips. "It's kind of a personal, legal matter," Nina whispered.

"Sadie?" Mr. Horowitz looked at his wife with a conspiratorial wink.

She smiled coyly and kissed Nina on the cheek. "Send my love to Natasia."

Mr. Horowitz and Nina walked into the living room and sat at the chess table near the fireplace.

"How about a game of chess?" he asked.

Nina smiled. "Not today."

"The only person under twelve years old who could beat me."

"Oh, you always let me win."

"Let you, not a chance. You're one sharp cookie." He waved his finger at her. "Do you still play?"

"I dabble."

"Okay. Good. Enough talk. What's going on?"

Nina's knees were trembling as she repeated the story.

"That's so horrible, Nina." He leaned towards her. "What in the world were you doing there?"

Nina started to cry.

He hugged her and patted her on the back.

"Didn't you know it was a troubled country?" he asked in a soft voice.

"Yes."

"And?"

21

She wiped her eyes with the back of her hand. "Amandine said we'd be completely safe. She said her father was an important business man in the country and we would be protected."

"So what changed?"

"She said she hadn't planned to get involved, but when her friends needed her, she felt she had to help."

"Nothing like a little rich girl searching for a cause, but why'd she mix you up in it?"

"I don't think she meant to." Nina looked down. "She was very insistent that I not come on the boat with her. I wanted to, but she told the fisherman to take me to the airport."

"You could have gotten in trouble."

"No. Everyone said they wouldn't be looking for me. I didn't have any problems at the airport."

"For all I did to get you asylum in this country and you almost wind up in a Haitian prison." He scratched his chin. "So you haven't heard from her?"

"No."

"Well if you do, she's going to need an attorney. Have you talked to anyone?"

"I asked Jim McNamara to help me and he laughed me out of his firm."

"Yeah, well this isn't quite his cup of tea." He made his eyebrows dance. "I can give you some names of attorneys who do this kind of work."

"The problem is, we don't have any money. I don't even think her father's supporting her tuition, anymore. This morning a new roommate showed up in my dorm."

He banged his hand on the chess table. "The injustice!"

"So what should I do? I promised I would help her."

"And you should."

"How?"

He scratched his chin and looked up to the ceiling for guidance. "Well hey, who needs money? Be your own lawyers. Help her prepare a case and have her represent herself." He whispered and looked at the ceiling again. Nina looked, too. There were a few cracks in the paint.

He waved his finger at her. "You don't need anyone to do anything for you if you can do it yourself. You're a cup, Nina. I told you. Do you remember what that means?"

Nina had heard it from him many times when she was growing up. "A smart head?"

"That's right. And that means you can do anything you want."

"You think so?"

He nodded vigorously with his lips puckered.

"Do you really think I could," she eyed him carefully, "prepare a case?"

"Oh, sure. I do think so."

"Well, what about court? I can't go to court if I'm not a lawyer."

"True. True."

She looked off in the distance. "Well, anyway, thanks for the ideas. I'll think of a way."

CHAPTER 3

Dressed in her most conservative outfit, a navy, turtleneck, khaki pants, moccasins and little lipstick, Nina entered her faculty advisor's office. She had played parts like this in theater class, prudent, studious, overly concerned about her future. Her long hair was pulled back into a yellow and pink polka dotted barrette.

Geri Korin, the advisor, looked up from her calendar. "Students have told me that Mr. Rupert's scene study class is a good one to take in your senior year. You know, it's a blow off." She emitted a raspy chuckle. "Would you like me to sign you up for an audition? I believe next Tuesday he's conducting auditions."

"I don't think I'll be taking any acting classes next semester," Nina said.

Geri looked at Nina's transcript and scratched her head. "Well, technically you still need six credits in acting to graduate with a major in Theater. You're required to finish these courses."

"I'm not required to do anything."

Geri gave little nervous pinches with her fingers to her forehead. "What is it that you would like to take next semester then?"

"Law."

"Why?"

"I want to go to law school."

"I don't understand."

"Do you need to?"

Geri flashed her a patronizing look.

"Look, forget it. I'll figure it out myself." Nina stood up, grabbed a packet for the law school application off of Geri's desk and darted out the door.

"Hey, wait a minute. I don't know what you think you're doing." Geri ran after her. "You can't get into law school now. Students prepare for years...the entrance exam is impossible. Come back here. Let's schedule your acting classes."

Nina ignored her, bounding for the exit, then spent the rest of the day lying on her belly, with a black pen clenched between her teeth, trying to tackle the application.

"It's no use," Nicholas said. "Even if by some miracle you got in, it would be way too late to help Amandine. By the way have you heard from her?"

"No."

Erica Axelrod

"Why don't you just let it go?" Nicholas said. "It's not your obligation to help her. No one else would do this."

"I promised I would get her a lawyer." She nibbled on the BLT on sourdough they had brought her from the coffee shop. She turned to Randy. "Don't you believe promises mean something?"

Randy skimmed through the application on her bed. "Yes, and I think your ideas are good, real good," he said. "But, it's a long shot."

"But she has passion and is intelligent," Nicholas chimed in, mockingly.

Later, they escorted her to the lobby with her papers. Nicholas gave Nina a hug, then Randy pecked her on the forehead with his lips. "Good luck, Nin. I hope you know what you're getting into."

Nina nodded with her lips pursed.

When they were gone, Nina sealed the application in a large envelope, licked the glue across the top and pressed the flap down with both index fingers. She put several stamps on without weighing it. Then she walked to the mailbox and tossed the application down the slot.

She made a dramatic show about it for Anthony, the guard in her dormitory.

"I'm going to law school," she told him. He sat on the wooden table in the entrance of the dorm every day wearing a blue, guard uniform. He knew the scoop on just about every student who lived in the building and tried to give the impression that he could be trusted with dark secrets. However, everyone knew Anthony was the

26

biggest gossip in town. He made life in New York City seem somehow, small.

Anthony shook his head. "Now hold on, you told me you was going to be a star."

"I am. Just a different kind of star."

"Oh, like a judge or something. Your Honor, Nina." He howled, staring down at Nina's feet that had black polish on the toenails and a toe ring on the right middle toe.

"I'm going to carve out my own niche, somewhere between a Supreme Court justice and, and Marilyn Monroe." She tilted her head back, posing.

"Good luck girl!"

"Thanks," Nina hopped up on the table next to Anthony and lit a cigarette.

A few sorority girls from outside on MacDougal Street began to pile in the front door. Nina looked at them as they signed their friends' names into the guest book. She had tried to be friends with these girls in her freshman year, but they had been indifferent to her.

"How come you never make me sign my guests into the book?" Nina asked puffing on her cigarette.

"Well, one time I did, and you rolled your eyes and was talking under your breath at me." He laughed out loud, then said, "Anyway, I know who you always bringing in here, that Randy or that Nicholas. Say, which one of them is your boyfriend anyway?"

Nina reached in her purse, pulling out some pictures of both of them. They were not in a wallet, rather, they were scattered around her purse along with photos of her Russian father and grandmother, opened lipsticks, loose change, gum wrappers with phone numbers, and some pens without caps. The pictures of Randy and Nicholas were torn around the edges. Nina held them up for Anthony to look at. "Which one do you think is my boyfriend?"

Anthony grabbed the photos and smoothed out the creases with his thumbs. Nicholas was playing guitar under a tree in one while Randy was drinking a beer in the other.

"I think you are datin' the college student." He pointed to Nicholas.

"No. I'm dating both of them. Shshsh." She put her finger to her lips.

"Seriously?"

"No." She laughed. "They are both just my friends."

He gave her a furtive look. "Well, I think that Nicholas has eyes for you. You better watch out for him."

She made her eyes dance, then skipped down the hall tossing her cigarette butt into the garbage can.

When she arrived at her room, broken glass was strewn across her floor. Nina looked behind the door. The full-length mirror was cracked in three places. At first, Nina thought she had been robbed, but then she saw chunks of a porcelain teacup in the middle of the slivers, as though someone had tossed the cup at the mirror. Nina looked over at Remmy's bed, it had been stripped naked. There was a note on the bed that said, "Nina, I can't do this law school thing." She left her phone number on the letter. It had a Connecticut area code. It said, "Call me if you need your improvisation notes."

Nina did not pick up the glass; instead, she swept the pieces to one side of the room so she would not cut her feet. Then she lay in bed, trying to figure out a plan, but could not concentrate. Her thoughts drifted to her friend on the wooden boat and the look in the eyes of her fellow refugees. She could still see their faces as if they were sitting next to her in the room.

The young girl with her hair loose and wild, like Nina, had caught her eye, then lay her head in Amandine's lap. Amandine was stroking her hair, telling her not to cry. She had worn a silk scarf around her neck and used it to pat her eyes.

The man seemingly in charge of the boat looked strong, with shapely biceps bulging as he pushed the boat out to sea. Confidently, he led a song in Creole, demonstrating hope and courage.

The instructor for the LSAT (Law entrance exam) course sat behind a desk inundated with finished mock exams. He had a red pen and was scribbling all over the tests with big X's.

"You're not going to get into law school with that score," he told Nina.

Nina rolled her eyes. For the last couple of weeks, she had sat in the back of his class and listened to him drone on about how difficult it was to get into law school. Then he said, even if the students did get into law school, only about sixty percent passed the New York Bar the first time and less than half the class would get employment as lawyers. His admonitions caused about five students to drop out of class to seek other professions. The instructor had been pleased.

"Look, this is just a practice test. I'll get into law school," Nina said.

"A thirty-two is not a good score. You need to be at least at thirty-nine for a decent law school to even look at you." The instructor threw Nina's paper in the wastebasket and started degrading the next student.

"It's not that bad," Nina heard a guy in her class say to her. "A thirty-two is not that bad. A friend of mine had lower than that on the practice test last year and he ended up acing the real exam. He's at Yale Law."

"How?"

"Meet me here tonight. We'll go over the tapes, do practice exams and grade each other," he offered.

"Why would you want to help me out?" Nina looked at him. "You don't even know me."

He stuck out his hand. "I'm Art Levin and I already know you're Nina."

Nina shook his hand while she stared at his red and white bow tie.

He fiddled with the tie and said, "Well, I just thought you needed some help and I, I...I thought we could be like a team, you know?"

"Okay." Nina smiled. "You got yourself a partner."

At the office, they spent from 6:00 p.m. to midnight, every night, studying for the LSAT. Art quizzed Nina and gave her inside tricks about logic games. The logic games would put forth scenarios like this: At a six person, rectangular table, Arlene sits head of the table, two seats from Eric, next to Betty, across from David, and Eric and Frank sit next to each other, where is Carol? (A) One seat from Arlene (B) Two seats from Arlene (C) Three seats from Arlene (D) None of the above (E) Not enough information to answer the question

Nina didn't get this problem until Art showed her how to approach each question methodically. He encouraged her to diagram a table on a piece of paper and fill in the spaces using the instructions one by one, trying the subjects in different points around the table. Nina followed his instructions until she finally figured out that Carol must be seated two seats from Arlene. Art taught Nina how to tackle each problem logically with a calculating eye as if she were playing chess. And by the end of the class, Nina and Art were both scoring one hundred percent on the logic games.

"We're doing awesome," Art told Nina. "What do you think?"

She sat back in the chair and put her feet up on the desk. "I think we need to go get a beer."

At the Beer Nook, around the corner from Hayden Hall, Art ordered a pitcher of beer and sat across from Nina in a wooden booth. "So why do you want to go to law school?" he asked.

"I've got my reasons."

He stared at her, but didn't ask for details. Then he paid the waiter for the beer and poured beer into each of their mugs. Nina watched as the foam toppled over the rim of the glass.

She chuckled. "Don't drink much beer, do you?"

Art looked up from his glass. He had a frothy mustache and he shook his head.

"So why do you want to go to law school?" she asked, then chugged down half of her beer.

He watched her as he spoke. "My dad. My dad is a doctor." He took off his glasses, breathed on the lenses, then wiped them with a beverage napkin. Nina could see little pieces of paper stuck to the lenses when he put the glasses back on.

"You see, he always wanted me to be a doctor, too. Well, I don't want to. I'm going to be the family's first lawyer." He swung his fists in the air.

"Wow! What a rebel!"

"Well, I am. My dad had me enrolled in summer science schools since I was eight."

"You should've become a dance teacher. Now that would've been rebellious."

"You're making fun of me. But you just don't understand. I'm finally taking a stand. I'm doing what I've always dreamed of. I want to be a judge someday."

Nina thought back to when Anthony had called her "Your Honor, Nina" and laughed at her black toenails. She poured another mug of beer. "Well, I bet you will someday. I bet you will. And your parents will be proud."

"No they won't. But it doesn't matter anymore," he whispered and looked around the room as if his father might be lurking around the table. "So now, you tell me, why is a theater major going to law school?"

She shook her head and sighed. "I'm sorry, but I don't wish to discuss this."

"I don't understand. How can going to law school be such a clandestine mission?"

She shrugged and gave Art a friendly kiss goodbye, then left him sitting alone in the booth with red lips tattooed on his cheek.

The classroom where the exam was administered was close to Nina's dorm so she woke up at 7:30 a.m. to arrive there by 8:00 a.m. She grabbed a raisin bagel and bottle of orange juice at the Village Coffee Shop on the way. Extra vitamin C, Randy told her, would give her brain a jump-start.

"You'll be in the room with the last names that start with the letters M through P." The monitor gave her the score sheet and question booklet. "You may proceed into the room and find an appropriate seat. Do not look at your question booklet until you're told."

Nina found a seat in the back; they were staggered so that no two students were sitting exactly next to each other. The students sat quietly, with solemn faces. Each had at least four, number two pencils and what appeared to be stacks of scrap paper. One student laid her watch out on the desk, starting a contagious reaction of other students doing the same. The students had less than a minute to complete each question. Nina had a single pencil, three pieces of blank paper and no watch.

Nina hadn't known what to expect. She was used to how the acting students behaved prior to an audition. She could remember them reciting their monologues, doing vocal warm-ups and practicing high kicks.

She wished that Art had been in her room. She had missed him by a few letters, though. He was in the H-L room next door. Nina knew Art would be at the front of the classroom with a bunch of blank paper and that he probably had his arms folded on his desk, looking very serious. Nina chuckled at the idea.

"Okay students, it's 8:33, you may begin."

Nina heard a panic of shuffling papers and moving chairs. She tried to ignore the clicking of the monitor's high heel shoes against the linoleum floor. It was distracting and rattled in her mind. Nevertheless, Nina remained composed as she went through each question in the method she and Art had practiced. She precisely filled in the circles of what she thought to be the best answers, then moved forward with nimble fingers. Nina put her pencil down at noon.

"How did it go?" Art looked up from his study materials. He was sitting in the hallway.

"I'm not sure. There's no way to tell."

"What are you talking about? Don't you remember the questions? Let's look up the answers you gave."

"Put that stupid study book away and let's go have lunch. It's pointless now."

"Did you have the questions with the table? It was just like we practiced," Art said as they sat down in Randy's section at the Village Coffee Shop.

"Yes, now let's not talk about it anymore. We can't change the outcome so forget it." Yet Nina grabbed his book and silently thumbed through the answers.

Nicholas slid into their booth. "Is this the same Nina who used to dance wild with me at the clubs on Saturday nights?"

Randy shrugged. "Man, I don't know." He lit a cigarette and sat down at their table.

In late October, Nina decided not to miss her improvisation class. She knew she couldn't skip it any longer because a failing grade could hinder her graduation. So reluctantly, she stood on the stage in Professor Pates' class and improvised a dramatic scene with another student. As she was pretending to cry, Professor Pates kept yelling, "Stronger, Nina, stronger. Come on. Get in touch with your emotions. What's happening to you?"

Nina moved to center stage and yelled, "I don't know. I'm not feeling it."

"Well then why don't you just go home today and stop wasting our time."

"Fine." She punched out a cardboard window on the set and left the room, banging her noisy clogs all the way to the door.

As she walked outside towards her dorm, she felt hollow, like a door inside of her was trying to close. She was thankful Remmy had not audited the class. Remmy would have pitied her and made her sweet, fruity tea.

Later that evening, Nina called Remmy and found out that Remmy was miserable in Connecticut. Her parents were nagging her to go back to law school before it was too late and her boyfriend, Kevin, had broken up with her. Before they hung up the phone, Remmy invited Nina to come out to Connecticut for the weekend.

The night before she left for Connecticut, she met her friends at Hugos in the East Village. It was a small pub that didn't allow women to enter until the 1970's. Now it was packed with an eclectic mix of college students.

Nina told the guys how she punched out the window on the set and stomped out of Professor Pates' class.

"You shouldn't do stuff like that. What if you don't get into law school?" Nicholas asked.

"Hey, nice talk. Nina's going to get into law school," Art said.

Randy changed the subject and offered everyone a shot of whisky. They did a round of shots as the volume in the pub began to escalate. People at the next table were chanting theme songs from television sitcoms.

Nina did some shots of licorice flavored whisky. The cough syrup taste swirled around her mouth and filled the empty pit of her stomach. Her body tingled with warmth and she felt giddy. She stood up on the table and did a tap dance in her clogs, and was quite enjoying the attention, until she looked into the crowd and saw an unfamiliar Haitian man edging towards her.

Nina leaped off the table and darted for the door. She bolted outside, but he was catching up with her, running close behind. When she turned the corner, she hid behind a green Volkswagen that was parked at the curb where she could catch her breath and take off her clogs. As she was removing her shoes, she saw his white tennis sneakers come near her and stop.

He crouched down to her level, staring at her face.

He was handsome, about her age, twenty-two.

"What do you want?" she said, shaking.

"I did not mean to scare you," he said. "I just wanted to get you alone." He extended his hand and put a small white card into her palm. "This is for you." He flashed a calming smile, then slipped around the corner.

Her hands trembling, she looked down at the card. It said, "Amandine made it to America."

She stood up, sprinting up and down the block looking for the man, but he seemed to have disappeared into the shadows of the trees.

"Are you okay?" Art asked, suddenly coming up behind her with Randy and Nicholas.

"There was a man." She pointed towards the trees. "Didn't you see him?"

"No. Where is he?" Randy asked, looking in every direction.

"He's gone now," she said, feeling dazed, yet euphoric. "Look, he gave me this." She handed the card to Randy, her hands trembling.

He looked down, reading. "This is wonderful."

Nina had tears in her eyes as she bear hugged Randy.

"But where'd the guy go?"

"He just disappeared."

"I wonder why he was so sneaky and was like chasing you?" Randy asked, strutting up and down the street.

"Maybe someone's after him," Nicholas said.

"What's going on?" Art asked.

"We'll explain later." Randy took Art aside. "Don't you live around the corner?"

"Yes. Just a few blocks."

"Is it okay if we take Nina there? She shouldn't walk home by herself."

"That's fine. Anything I can do."

In the morning, Nina awoke to the aroma of hazelnut coffee.

She slowly walked into Art's living room. She rubbed her eyelids with her fingers and focused on Art. He was sitting at a table studying and sipping coffee.

"Good morning," she said quietly.

He looked up. "Good morning. How did you sleep?"

"Awesome." She stretched her arms, reaching above. "It feels so wonderful to finally know that my friend is okay." She moved to the couch, pushing away Art's blanket and pillow. "Hey, I'm sorry you had to sleep on the couch."

"Oh, it was nothing. Can I get you some coffee?"

Nina nodded.

Art brought her gourmet coffee in a mug that listed famous Arts. Arthur Miller and Arthur Murray were the only names she recognized.

"Someday, Art Levin will be on a mug," Nina said as she sipped the hot coffee.

"Not me. You'll be the famous one my friend."

"For what?"

"Oh, maybe tap dancing on tables." He winked at her.

"Hey, that was pretty good. I had the crowd going. For a little while anyway." She giggled, nestling herself into the cushions of the sofa.

"It's unbelievable what happened to you in Haiti."

She nodded.

"Well, it sounds like things might be okay for your friend. And look, now you have a bright future ahead of you."

"How so?"

"Well, I think you're going to be a terrific lawyer someday. You're intelligent, you have spice and you'd stun any jury."

"Why?"

"Well, look at you. You're beautiful."

Nina helped herself to the shower. When she was finished, she asked Art if she could borrow his clothes. As she was standing there all wet, she stuck her arm out of the bathroom door to grab the jeans and white oxford that he fished through the crack. She slipped on the clothes and walked barefoot towards the couch. Although Art was fairly skinny, she was drowned in his clothes. Art gave her a bag from the bookstore to tote her belongings. She could smell smoke and beer on her clothes as she stuffed them into the bag. Then she slipped on her clogs and coat, thanked Art and gave him a peck on the cheek.

Nina grabbed a bagel and orange juice at a Korean delicatessen, then went to Washington Square Park. It was unusually beautiful weather for late October. She sat down at a bench by the chess players, removed her coat and nibbled a bagel with cream cheese.

"Uh oh, the Russian is here," a player named Charlie said. "I'm challenging you next girl." He pointed to Nina.

"What? Is she good?" another man asked.

"You don't know?"

The man shook his head.

Charlie leaned in towards the men. "Why, she's the chess princess around here. She can beat just about anybody. It's in her Russian blood."

The men all stared at her. She finished her bagel, wiped off the crumbs from her hands and sat down in front of Charlie.

She put her two knights out first, then set up her queen behind her bishop. She was on the offensive at the start. Old Charlie kept a good defensive strategy, but he just couldn't manage to keep control. Nina conquered his queen, then got both rooks in the two back rows and old Charlie was gone. These guys were sophisticated players; they didn't even bother to call checkmate. They knew when their time had come. Charlie stood up, another man moved into Charlie's position and Nina began again.

Nina controlled the game, but when no one could beat her, she got bored. She spied Nicholas watching her from the sidelines so she left her winning seat and walked towards him.

"You're amazing. I've been watching you for about twenty minutes," Nicholas said. "I didn't know." He put his arm around her. "By the way, what're you wearing?"

She laughed. "Art's clothes."

"Nice." He winked.

They walked towards the fountain. He played some classic tunes on his guitar while both he and Nina sang. Shortly after, a crowd formed around them. Nina removed her clogs and instigated a hacky sack with her feet. The ground felt warm beneath her toes on this particularly warm, October day.

They hung around in the park until noon.

At noon, office workers crowded the park with their packed lunches. Nina kneed the hacky sack to Nicholas who bounced it off of his head and into a woman, causing her to drop her papers. Nina helped the woman pick up her stack and noticed that there was a letter from the testing center where the LSAT was administered. The woman received a score of thirty-five. She saw Nina staring at her score and grabbed the paper out of Nina's hand.

Leaving her clogs behind, she sprinted to her dormitory. "Results are in!" She told Anthony who was sitting on the guard table as usual.

"Where you been girl, dressed like that?" He was staring at her feet and Art's outfit.

Nina smiled. "Ooh! I'll never tell."

She raced to her mailbox and there it was. Her future wrapped in a lifeless, flimsy little envelope. She took it out of the box, running her fingers over it. She tried to peek through the plastic as she sat on the corner of Anthony's desk. "Well, here it goes," she said, ripping open the top of the envelope and pulling out the score sheet. There was a whole bunch of information, then in bold letters in the middle of the page was the number forty-six.

Nina's hands trembled. She stared at the number in disbelief. She raced to the bathroom and was trying to catch her breath in the first stall.

Anthony was banging on the door. "Are you okay in there? Nina! You okay?"

Nina wiped her face and forced herself to calm down. She sucked water from the tap, then came back out. "I'm fine. I just got a little nervous. I'm going to be a lawyer."

"Yeah, so. You've told me that already. Your Honor, Nina." He laughed for a moment, then handed her a can of soda pop and made her sit down until she was calm.

The first person she called was her mother at her studio in Florida. The phone rang six times, before Natasia answered.

"Nina, how are you? I have not heard from you. Why have you not called?" She spoke in a Russian accent.

"I'm calling now. Listen, I've got some very important news."

"What is it? Don't tell me you are pregnant. I cannot handle that right now. You know your father, he is coming."

"Are you serious?"

"Yes. He just needs his papers in order."

"Maybe I can help him."

"That is very nice, but we need a lawyer. So?"

"So what?"

"So what is your important news?"

Nina sat down in the phone booth, putting her bare feet against the door window. "I've changed my mind. I don't want to be an actress anymore."

"Good. That is a miserable life."

"Now you tell me."

"So? What do you want to be?"

"It's not what I want to be. It's what I'm going to be."

"Well, what is it? What is it?"

"I'm going to law school." Nina breathed out some air she had been holding.

"Law school?" Natasia was quiet for a second. "How could you go to law school? You don't know about the law. You have only studied acting."

"Well, that's what I thought, too. But this is America, remember? I can be anything I want to be."

"Ha! Then come help me teach the tango in Florida."

Nina laughed. "I'm serious. I've taken a law entrance exam and got an almost perfect score. I can go to any law school I want."

"This is too much. It cannot be."

"Yes, it can. It can."

"And money? How can you afford this?"

"Loans. The government gives full loans, just like college."

"And you can pay it back?"

"Of course. I'm going to be a lawyer."

"Wow!" Natasia screamed, jubilantly. "My Nina. My little Nina, she is going to be a lawyer." Nina heard her mother shout over the music to some friends in her dance class.

Later that day, Nina paid a visit to advisor, Geri Korin. Geri looked at her score.

"Well, with this score, I can't believe it, I bet you, yes you, can get into any school you like." She gave a raspy laugh. "I can't believe this."

Dinner in Connecticut with Remmy and her family had been set upon a long, Victorian table with bouquets of roses arranged in crystal vases. Bottles of wine, liqueur and Scotch were poured in proper drinking vessels, and a turkey was beautifully presented on a silver tray surrounded by garlands of vegetables that were only for show.

Servants rustled back and forth with five courses, but the diners politely pushed their food around plates. Nina barely knew Remmy, but guessed that when the door was closed, Remmy would stuff her mouth with mounds of chocolate. Now, she sat sedately in front of a heaping plate of pomme soufflé, taking tiny forkfuls.

Remmy was seated second to the right of her grandfather, Harold Peterson, who sat head of the table. He was a plump man, with white hair and a ruddy complexion. Remmy told Nina that his hair had once been the color orange so when he became senior partner at the Peterson law firm, the employees all called him the "Heat Miser" from the Christmas television special. Nina could still see some orange hairs protruding behind the white, resembling an orange ice pop with cream in the center.

Nina sat in between Remmy and her brother, Steve. Steve was a new lawyer who had recently graduated from the University of Pennsylvania and had just passed the New York Bar. He wore khakis and a dress shirt with no tie. He had a square jaw that outlined a handsome face. Remmy had told Nina that he was expected to replace Harold someday as senior partner in the Peterson law firm. Their father was an orthopedic surgeon who had his own successful practice.

When the room was completely quiet, Remmy was the first to break the silence. "Grandfather, guess what my friend Nina here got on the LSAT?"

Harold put down his fork sideways on top of his plate, carefully chewed whatever food was left in his mouth and then directed his attention toward Nina. In fact, all parties at the table were focused on Nina, patiently waiting for an answer. Nina thought about the LSAT problem. If Harold was sitting next to Remmy's mother, Laney Peterson, and Laney was next to Remmy, who would be on the other side of Remmy?

She swallowed a large chunk of turkey so she would not be chewing when it was her turn to speak. She choked a little, then managed a response. "Oh, it was nothing really. Well, I guess it was quite good. Yes, um, I got a forty-six." Nina's hands were trembling for some reason. She noticed that Steve was staring at her, affectionately.

Harold's eyebrow's raised in arcs. He jiggled the ice in his glass of Scotch and took a sip while studying Nina. "Well, that's quite remarkable." He cleared his throat while the other people at the table waited to hear what he would say next.

Nina thought about the community in Brooklyn where she had grown up, how they all talked at once, but no one ever really listened to each other.

"Um, Steve." He cleared his throat. "What do you think of that? Do you know anyone else who has gotten a forty-six?"

Steve wiped his mouth. "I don't think so." He turned to look at Nina. "With a score like that you can go to any school you'd like."

Nina stared back at him. They were right next to each other and the rest of the table seemed to have disappeared momentarily. She breathed in his cologne. "I want to go to NYU."

"Good school." He winked at her.

The rest of the room remained quiet.

Nina felt her pulse beating. "So um, did you like law school?"

He laughed. "Let's just say I find the study of law very interesting, but I think the practice of law is very different."

Nina could see Steve exchange glances with his grandfather.

"How so?" she asked.

"You see, the practice of law is more about billing hours than it is about legal theories."

Everyone laughed until Steve's mother, Laney, interrupted. "Nina, Steve has just joined the family's law firm and hasn't quite gotten used to the billing process."

Steve smiled uncomfortably. "No. It's not that I'm not used to it. I just don't agree with it."

"And what is it that you don't agree with?" Harold raised his voice.

"Well, I just don't care for some of the practices. Like, billing people a hundred dollars for calling to ask a question."

"Well, it depends on what kind of question." Harold laughed along with the rest of the people at the table.

Steve turned towards Nina. "Make sure that when you choose an area to practice law that you really believe in what you're doing." He beamed fondly, picked up his plate and escaped into the kitchen.

Nina's face was flushed, and there was an awkward silence until Harold cleared his throat and changed the subject. "So Nina, have you accepted any offers yet?"

She cocked her head to try to peek into the small round window on the kitchen door to see if she could see Steve. Remmy nudged her in the side with her elbow.

"Offers? You mean with a firm?"

Harold laughed. "Yes. Have you accepted an offer with a firm?"

"Well, I haven't even gone to law school yet."

"You'll need to do an internship with a good firm your first summer out. You be sure to call me and set something up," Harold said.

Nina nodded, affecting a smile.

Later on, as Nina and Remmy looked at old photo albums in Remmy's bedroom, Nina whipped through the pages looking for Steve. He had really curly hair when he was little that was sandy blonde. Now, it was darker and only curled a little in the back. In the picture, he was having a birthday party. He was riding on a pony next to several other children. Remmy was sticking her tongue out at him. Nina chuckled. "So what was that all about with Steve and your grandfather?"

"Oh, that. Who knows? I think Steve thinks he's like some morality expert."

"Why?"

"Well, he's, like, always talking about noble ideas and dreams of making a difference. Meanwhile, he's

48

next in line in the family law firm and his trust fund kicks in at the first of the year."

Nina looked at the photo of Steve's smiling face. "I think it's really neat that someone in his position would have such integrity."

Remmy squinted so her eyebrows moved closer to the center of her forehead. "Hey, don't start getting designs for my brother because he would never be available to you."

"Excuse me? What's that supposed to mean?"

"Well, come on. You're not exactly refined. I mean you look kind of, like, a bimbo."

"Why? Why are you saying this to me?"

"Well, hey come on. I don't mean to get you upset. I'm just saying that my brother isn't supposed to waste his time with a girl, without, you know?"

"No, I don't know."

"Connections, a good name. That's the type of girl that Steve is supposed to marry."

"According to who?"

"My family. Who do you think?"

Nina stared down at Remmy's silk blanket that was across her canopy bed. Nina still slept with the same blanket she had since she was ten. It had those little lint balls all over it from being washed too many times.

"Look, I think it's stupid, too. That's why I kind of rebelled and left law school. I mean, and then I spent all that time doting over Kevin, a nobody, but it was fun."

"I think you thought Kevin was more than fun. He broke up with you."

Remmy grabbed the photo album from Nina and put it back on her shelf. "So what're you trying to say?"

"I'm not trying to say anything. You're the one who started this ridiculous conversation. I can't believe I came out to visit you. I had no idea how shallow you were." Nina fumed, then left Remmy's room and went to the bathroom. She slammed the door and took a hot shower. As she conditioned her long hair, she tried to run her fingers through and disentangle it. She yanked and pulled on it vehemently. Then she sat on the toilet in front of the mirror brushing it out and crying.

When Nina returned to NYU after the visit, she received a letter:

Dear Nina,

I am so sorry if I have offended you in anyway. I guess I was just jealous that my brother and grandfather paid special attention to you. They never give one lick of attention to me. Please forgive me.

My parents have begged me to try school again before it's too late. I'm bored here so I guess I'll come back and hang out.

I have pretty much gotten over Kevin.

Well, I hope you will forgive my ignorance. I think you are the most beautiful person I know.

Love, Remmy

Nina folded the letter and placed it in her shoebox with other letters, mostly letters from her grandmother that Nina could not understand. She had never gotten them translated and she had forgotten her Russian language long ago.

She thought about the strange night at Remmy's house. Remmy had so insulted her and she had sat in the bathroom and cried. Remmy had banged on the door, but Nina had refused to unlock it.

Finally, Steve had jimmied open the door and they found Nina sitting on the toilet seat, naked, brushing her hair.

Steve had gazed at Nina momentarily, his face flushed, then grabbed a monogrammed towel from the rack to cover her. After he left, Remmy sat next to Nina on the floor of the bathroom and they both cried.

A few days later as Nina was waiting for Remmy to come back to school, Anthony knocked on the door.

"You've got a call girlfriend."

"Who is it?" She peeked through the crack.

"Amandine."

She hurdled over the steps, two at a time, then slipped into the phone booth and shut the door.

"Amandine," Nina cried. "Is it really you?"

"Yes, my friend. We made it."

"Oh this is wonderful. I just knew you would." She clasped her hands together, giving a silent prayer of gratitude.

"Well it's really not so wonderful. This is no life. I'm living in the back of some old house with other refugees, afraid to go outside for fear that the INS will pick me up."

"Where are you?"

"Somewhere in Miami, Little Haiti."

"I'm coming down there."

"No, please. I do not need any attention."

"Well what can I do?"

"Well, I told you I would need a lawyer, but now I do not have access to any money. You see, the Refugee Clinic called NYU and determined that I am no longer enrolled as a student. I am certain the officials in my government made my father pull me out." She paused, catching her breath. "The attorney at the clinic told me that now my student visa will be invalid and although I've been studying here for most of my life, I have no legal right to be here."

"Are you well? What have you been eating?"

"Rice and beans, plantains, most of what we eat back home. The woman who is keeping us is very nice, but this is no life."

"Well, did you tell the lawyer at the clinic your story?"

"Yes, and he says I have a good case for political asylum, but there are so many refugees and they do not have enough resources to process every claim." She talked very fast as if she was running out of time. "Right now, they are trying to round up law schools to send their students to help."

"Law students?"

"Yes."

"That's wonderful. I'm going to law school next year."

"You are what?"

"Yes. I promised you I would get you a lawyer, but I couldn't. So I applied to law school."

"You would do that for me?"

"Of course. You are my best friend."

Nina could hear her crying softly.

"I love you Nina. You are the best of all friends. You are true."

That night, Remmy came back and she was unpacking all of her conservative suits and dresses on embroidered hangers and carefully placing them in the closet.

"Aren't these ugly?" she said. "This is what I have to wear to be a liar." They laughed,

Nina rummaged through them, giddy with bubbly laughter. She held a pin-stripe suit in front of her. "What do you think?"

"Never."

Nina threw it down on the bed and made them some coffee. "Well, it's good to have you back. I was kind of lonely by myself."

Remmy took her coffee and sat on her bed. "So did you ever find out what happened to your other roomy?"

Nina looked down. "I don't want to talk about it."

"Come on, please. Maybe I can help."

Nina looked at her, coming up with an idea. "Well, maybe you can." She sat next to her and confided in her the details of the story about Amandine.

"That's unreal. And you were there?"

"Yes. Unfortunately."

"My life is so boring compared to that."

"That's good. Trust me."

"So how can I help?"

Nina stood up, pacing, rubbing her chin like Mr. Horowitz always did, thinking maybe she could massage some wisdom into her brain. "You're a law student now. Maybe you can help to process her claims and then when I become a law student, I can take over. It's a lengthy process."

Remmy swished the coffee around her mouth. "You must live in some kind of a bubble. Have you not noticed this past semester I have yet to attend a class?"

"So your status is just a formality. I'll do the work."

"How would you know how? You don't know the first thing about the law."

"Well, maybe I can attend some of your classes. You know just to get an idea."

"Be my guest."

CHAPTER 4

Professor Maddock paced back and forth in front of a full classroom of first year law students in a Property class before clearing his throat and speaking. "Ms. Pinto, stand up and state the facts of <u>Pierson v. Post</u>."

Ms. Pinto stood up next to her chair, eloquently reciting the facts as if she had written them herself.

After class, Nina ran to use the phone. "Remmy, you better start going to class. These people know everything and there are tons of notes to be taken. You're never going to make it if you don't start coming to class."

She heard Remmy laughing and flirting with some guy in the background.

"Nina. If you're so interested, why don't you just go and lake the notes for me."

"Well I can, but the professors randomly call on people. What if they call on me?"

"I don't know. You can pretend you're me. No one's ever met me."

"That's highly unethical."

"Well, it's not like I'm asking you to take my tests for me. You don't get graded on class participation anyway. Grading is all based on final exams and it is completely anonymous."

"I don't know."

"Hey, it's for your friend." She giggled to some guy in the background, telling him to buy her a Diet Coke. "Hey, you can borrow some of my stuffy clothes."

Nina bought a red wig, then put it on her head and did it up in a bun. Then she bought some thick black glasses with dark tinting that practically covered her entire face. Finally, she borrowed Remmy's clothes that were four sizes big and she had to pad it. She wore no lipstick and looked nothing like herself.

Later, she went to the library and sought a cubicle close to four girls in Remmy's class. She eavesdropped on their conversation with Joseph Dewey, an older student.

"Look, it's just a big head game. Don't sweat it. By your third year here, you'll have your feet up on the desk and when a professor calls on you, you won't answer his question. Instead, you'll say, professor, I pass!" Dewey said. "Okay, let's say it altogether. 'Professor. I pass.'"

The girls laughed and repeated his words.

"What junk!" Nina said, continuing to watch Dewey's melodrama. When he heard her comment, he swaggered over to her cubicle and placed his hand on her shoulder.

She immediately pushed it off. "Do you mind?" She made her voice deeper, using a technique she had recently learned in a voice class.

"I never mind," he answered with a toothy smile, then plopped down, backwards, on a chair. "I haven't seen you here before. What's your name?"

She cleared her throat to get ready to begin the charade. "Remmy. Remmy Peterson." She extended her hand.

He shook it lightly. "The Remmy Peterson, the grand kid of the Peterson empire?"

She nodded.

"Well, no wonder you don't study. You're the heir to the throne." He had gales of laughter. "Hey, if you need help catching up, I'm the king of procrastination."

"Nice to know."

He patted her on the head and sauntered off to the next group of girls.

He had black hair cut in a trendy surfer style. He wore his jeans cuffed at the bottom with holes in the knee and an Oxford that hung to his thighs. He sported a white T-shirt underneath his Oxford and high tops with the laces untied.

"I just don't understand what he's doing in law school," the guy next to her said as he tapped at his ear with the eraser on the bottom of his pencil. "He's not at all interested in the study."

Nina shrugged. "Well, everyone's different."

"I think I'm in your Civil Procedure class. Professor Lynn Wiley?"

Nina nodded, not sure.

"She calls on you all the time and makes comments about your absence. Are you going to her class today?"

"I'm not sure."

"Well don't mind her if she's hard on you. She's a little tough." He bent his arm to make a muscle and puckered his lips.

"How so?"

"Well, she bawled me out for failing to brief a case on the first day of school," he said. "Look, briefing cases is getting really monotonous. Do you think we could do it together?"

"Well, to tell you the truth, I really don't know how to brief cases."

"No? You better learn or Wiley is going to humiliate you." He pulled up close to her, giving her a lesson. "Look, it's really very simple. Facts, well, that's just a summary of what happened. Issue is the question for the court, usually begins with the word 'whether;' and that's not rain or snow."

Nina gave an obligatory laugh as she watched Dewey knock his unopened can of soda pop on the floor near Nina's leg. He picked it up and ran over to the window where he opened it over the ledge. Nina watched as it exploded into a carbonated fizz.

Her first day in Civil Procedure class, Professor Lynn Wiley reminded the class that their presentations were due tomorrow. "Who would like to go first?" She gazed around the room. Nina shrunk down into her chair, trying not to be noticed, but Wiley looked right at her.

"And who might you be?"

She cleared her throat. "Remmy, Remmy Peterson," she said quietly.

"Ah, Ms. Peterson. Welcome. I'm so glad you decided to join us. Because you see your granddaddy will not be with you during exam time." She had one hand on her hip and used the other to toss chalk in the air. "Why don't you present your assignment tomorrow?"

"What is it?"

"You must demonstrate a presentation of faulty service of process in a federal case."

Wiley snickered as she wrote Remmy Peterson on the blackboard under tomorrow's presentation. Nina felt a bit sickened by the predicament she was getting herself into, but she kept telling herself it was for a good cause and the charade would be over soon.

Nina spent the rest of the day in the library, learning all about the Federal Rules of Civil Procedure, taking only one break to go to an acting class and have lunch at the Village Coffee Shop. During lunch, she solicited Randy to get her plastic pinafores, affectionately dubbed pinneys by sports enthusiasts. Randy had been a soccer coach for his nephews in Brooklyn and had much old equipment lying around his apartment. Around dinner time, Nina went to the vending machine to purchase some candy bars. Then as she was drinking from the water fountain, someone came up behind her and grabbed her arm.

Nina whipped around. Remmy was standing there, grinning. "I would like some research done on the laws of love." She howled, pushing Nina into one of the stacks. Nicholas followed behind them.

"What're you guys doing?"

"We're going to Hugos for a beer. Come with us; you're taking this way too seriously," Remmy said.

"Hello. I have a presentation to prepare for."

"You mean I have a presentation to prepare for." Remmy was hysterical as she pulled a bottle of wine out of her overcoat, took a sip and passed it to Nicholas.

"How do you two even know each other?" Nina asked.

"I was coming to visit you, when Remmy greeted me in a black spandex dress. Whoa!"

"You're wearing my dress?" Nina asked Remmy.

"Hey, spandex stretches and you're wearing mine." She slouched down, swigging the wine.

"Give me that." Nina grabbed the bottle. "This is a library."

"See I told you," she said to Nicholas. "A couple of days in this place and she has already lost her sense of humor."

"I have fine humor, but I have work to do."

"Fine then. Here's your pinneys." Nicholas handed her a brown paper bag. "What're you going to do, play soccer? Nina's a dynamite hackey sack player," he said to Remmy.

Nina ignored him, looking inside the bag, counting the pinneys. Randy had come through. There were ten red pinneys and ten blue pinneys. "Thank you."

Nina said good-bye and left them sitting in the stacks and went back to her work. She was preparing a scenario where the law students would have to enact a live improvisation. The students with the red pinneys would act as refugees fleeing from the INS. The students in the blue pinneys would be INS officers. They would have to try to tag the refugees and hand them with a summons of deportation proceedings. They had no names or addresses and were generic summons that are not allowed for proper service of process. She would also assign one student to be a photographer to take pictures of the scene. She would give the student a water gun camera. Finally, she bought three flashlights to give to the officers. She planned on making the classroom dark.

As Nina was preparing her faulty summons, she was interrupted by what sounded like hyenas. She looked up and saw Dewey dancing with some law books on his head. He was entertaining a group of freshmen girls that were in her class. Nina placed her hands over her ears and continued to read the case.

"Hey, what's your problem? Why are you such a party pooper?" Dewey popped himself up on Nina's desk and pulled her hands away from her ears.

"Look, I'm trying to prepare for an assignment here. This is supposed to be a library."

"Oh, come on. We're just having some fun. Law school doesn't have to be miserable."

"I don't think it's miserable. I find it interesting."

"Strange. Must be genetic."

"Look, if you don't find it interesting, why are you wasting your time here?" Nina looked over at the girls. They were walking across the floor, trying to balance the casebooks on their heads. It was late, about midnight.

"To make lots of money!" Dewey answered.

"Who cares if you have a lot of money, if you don't enjoy what you do?"

"I do." He roared. "Hey, lighten up. A bunch of us are getting a beer at the Sticky Suds. Why don't you come?"

"I pass."

"Why?"

"I have to prepare."

"Suit yourself," he said, then strutted back to the table. Nina watched as the group put on their coats and exited the library. Nina kept focused on her case, isolated in her cubicle until 2:00 a.m.

The next day, Nina stood up at the doorway and passed out pinneys, flashlights and summons to the students as they entered the classroom. She chose a student named Marcy Weiner, one of Dewey's friends, to be the photographer. When all students had entered the class and the door was closed, Nina moved to the lectern to begin her presentation.

"Ladies and Gentlemen, you are about to participate in a live improvisation. Red pinneys stand up." Some of the students hustled to their feet while others seemed reluctant to join her presentation. "Red pinneys, you are refugees fleeing to America. It is your job to create a truthful scene. Come forward please." They slowly walked to the front of the class. "Now, close your eyes and try to imagine what it would be like to flee for your life. Try to imagine how it would feel and let your natural actions guide you."

"What is this, an acting class?" one student said.

"Just do what she says," Wiley responded.

Nina smiled. "Blue pinneys stand up." This time the students seemed more responsive after Wiley had supported her. "Blue pinneys, you are the INS. It is your job to catch these refugees and tag them with your summons. You can stay in your seats until the lights go out."

"Lights go out?"

"Three of you have flashlights. Use them."

"What am I supposed to do with this camera?" Marcy Weiner asked.

"You are the reporter. It is your job to take pictures."

"This is a water gun."

"Yes, it squirts just a drop. Pick three important photo ops and pull the trigger." She looked at the students with the red pinneys. "If you get sprayed with

63

the camera, you must freeze. You are going to be used as a live photograph."

"Wow. Cool."

Wiley headed up the stairs towards the doorway, pausing a moment. "Ready, go," she said, shutting the light.

The law students that were usually stiff in their seats were now running up and down the stairs in the amphitheater-like-classroom, leaping over chairs, toppling one another and laughing.

"Two more minutes," Nina said, staring at the clock.

All the refugees were tagged and handed the summons. Three were in frozen positions. Nina climbed the stairs and turned on the light. "You can stop. Take a seat on the floor wherever you are. Except the photograph people. You remain frozen." The students listened and motion was halted.

Nina grabbed the summons out of each of the hands of the red pinneys and walked to the front of the room where she addressed Wiley. "Your Honor, these summons are faulty. They do not have a name or address on them and were handed to these refugees in a generic manner. This service of process violates the Federal Rules of Civil Procedure and these refugees should be dismissed from custody."

Wiley smiled, deep in thought. Then walked towards Nina. "But counselor, your clients are not American citizens. They may not be afforded the same constitutional rights as a citizen." She looked at the class. "Look that one up."

Nina sat on the closest desk, arms folded. "Then your Honor, in the alternative, I would like to plead political asylum for these refugees who came to America fleeing for their lives."

"I see, and what evidence do you have?" Wiley asked.

Nina walked in front of the live photographs, pointing to each one. "I have photographs here demonstrating that these refugees were fleeing for their lives in fear of persecution."

Wiley walked by each live photograph, seemingly to examine them, nodding her head, then looked at Nina. "Asylum granted."

"Thank you, your Honor. I only wish it was this easy."

Overall, the students were in good humor over Nina's exercise, except for Marcy Weiner who had accidentally opened the stopper of the water gun and had gotten soaked.

When the bell rang, students came up to Nina to shake her hand and congratulate her on her presentation. As the classroom emptied, Wiley came from behind her lectern and stood in front of Nina's chair.

"Ms. Peterson, that was quite a presentation. However, next time, let's do without the water."

Nina's stomach turned. "I'm sorry. I didn't mean to cause..."

"No. Don't apologize. It was a most clever presentation. I especially liked the pinneys." She chuckled, then looked at Nina more seriously. "How would you like to be my research assistant?"

Nina's feet felt light under her legs. She was getting deeper into this every day, but a research assistant could have access to many legal resources and she needed to learn about the Federal Rules of Civil Procedure for Amandine's case. "I would love to." Nina gave a crafty smile.

"Um, I have just one question."

"Okay," Nina said, hoping she wouldn't ask about her personal background.

"Why did you skip the first two months of class?"

Nina looked down at Wiley's feet. She wore royal blue pumps to match her royal blue dress and royal blue eye shadow.

"I was nervous of failure." Nina answered the way she thought the real Remmy would.

"Look, I think you've got what it takes to be a great lawyer." Wiley gave a gracious smile. "You've got gumption, kiddo."

"Finals are next week."

"Come again?" Remmy said. She and Nicholas had dual headsets and were jamming to some music on a Walkman in their room. Remmy was singing out loud.

Nina went over to her and took off her headphones. "I'm not taking your finals for you. I will not go that far."

"Why not?"

"Because, today I found out I was officially accepted to law school next year and I'm excited about it."

"Well, good for you," Remmy said, sitting up on Nicholas' lap. He was playing with her hair.

"Look all I wanted to do was audit some classes, and now I'm Remmy Peterson, Lynn Wiley's research assistant." Nina rubbed her hands through her long blonde hair. It felt good to have her wig off.

"You're a research assistant?" Nicholas took off his headphones. "How did that happen?"

"I don't know. I'm not sure how any of this happened, but I don't want to get in trouble. I'm not taking your tests."

Remmy walked over to Nina and put her arm around her.

"Nina, you're already in great trouble if you get caught. Taking my tests won't make a bit of difference." She stuffed a piece of chocolate in her mouth. "Besides, I can't very well just show up on exam day now. They're going to be like, who is this?"

"You should have thought about that before." Nina grumbled. "I'm done. I'm done being Remmy Peterson."

"What am I supposed to do?"

"Just withdraw. You don't want to be a lawyer anyway. Just withdraw and go do something else. That's the only way out of this."

"I'll lose my trust fund."

"You should have thought of that before. I mean, you didn't expect me to be Remmy Peterson all through law school did you?"

"I don't know what I expected." She bit her red fingernails. "This is getting pretty hairy."

"I have a solution girls," Nicholas said, rocking on his heels. They sat on either side of him and listened. "Remmy needs to stay in law school, but she can't go back to NYU because everyone will know that someone else was pretending to be her. And she doesn't want to withdraw altogether because she will lose her trust fund. So why doesn't she just transfer to a new school?"

"Good idea. How about Miami? Then you'll be near Amandine," Nina said.

"I'm not going to Miami. I'd miss Nicky." She sat on his lap again and gave him a kiss.

Nina rolled her eyes. "I can't believe what I'm dealing with here."

Just then, there was a knock on the door. "Hey Nina, open up, you've got a phone call."

"Hello."

"Nina, it's Amandine."

"Amandine, honey, how are you?"

"Awful. The house we were staying in was raided last night. I'm in the Detention Center and they are filing deportation proceedings against me. I need help immediately."

"I'll be there as soon as possible."

Nina found the number for the Refugee Clinic in Miami and asked for the director, Wess Salinger.

"You've got to let me come down there and help to process my friend's papers."

"I told you, Ms. Peterson, we don't allow first year law students to do this work."

"Why?"

"Because we don't know what kind of work they can do yet. And we'll only have the best for our clients."

"I'm top of my class."

"You haven't taken exams yet."

"I'll ace them. I'll show you."

On Thursday nights, the law students attended a different bar in the city for a social hour. In mid-December, Nina attended the party for the first time. It was at a sports bar on the Upper East Side. The students who were normally ensconced with several law books in cubicles at the library were now carefree and sipping beers from various, expensive labels. Nina ordered vodka with a splash of cranberry.

Nina only attended the party because she had completed the final exams. Professor Lynn Wiley had urged Nina to accompany her. The women sipped their drinks while discussing legal issues at a private table. Nina inquired about rules of evidence as she recorded Wiley's responses with a small, cassette player that was in her pocket.

"Professor Wiley, can I ask you a question about evidence?"

Wiley nodded.

"Okay, if you wanted to introduce, say, a photograph into evidence, what would be the proper procedure?" Nina asked.

"Well, first you would call the photographer as a witness and you would try to lay a foundation for the photograph by asking the photographer whether or not he or she took the picture."

"And what if the photographer is unavailable?"

"I don't see that happening because of subpoena rights unless he was out of the country or something." Wiley sipped on a glass of Chablis. Her fingernails were colored red, but Nina could tell that Wiley polished them herself.

"Okay, assume he's out of the country."

"Then you would have to go another route."

Nina listened as she fished in her coat pocket for her tape recorder. She pressed the record button without flinching as she had done so many times. After Nina taped Wiley's answers, she went home and typed out the responses on an old, black Royal typewriter that her mother had given to her. When Nina was finished, she placed her notes in organized flies.

Wiley continued. "You would have had to obtain the photographs from somewhere. Perhaps, a third party has found the photographs and has submitted it to counsel during the investigation. You could call that person to the stand, ask him to verify where he or she found the photographs and that person could lay the foundation. Then you simply ask the court to introduce the photographs into evidence marked as an exhibit. When the judge approves, then the evidence is marked and the jury can look at them."

Click. Nina shut the recorder. "Thank you. You're always so helpful."

"It's my job."

Nina excused herself to go to the bathroom so she could test the recording. She looked under the stalls, and when she saw they were empty, played back the tape. It was perfect. She fixed her barrette to hold up her bun, then walked back towards her table. She ran into Joseph Dewey on her way.

"How's Ms. Peterson tonight?" Dewey stretched his arm around Nina's neck, pulling her close while his group of admirers looked on. Marcy Weiner was still incensed over having to wear wet clothes all day after Nina's presentation.

"I'm doing quite well, thank you."

"Can I buy you a drink?"

"Vodka with a splash of cranberry, as long as there are no strings attached." Nina smiled demurely and headed back towards the professor.

"Must have been a long line for the bathroom. Should I wait till later?" Wiley asked as she studied Nina.

"Yes, that would be a good idea."

Dewey pushed his way into the booth next to Nina. "Here's your vodka." He lit a cigarette and offered one to Nina. Nina shook her head no. She had quit smoking recently.

"How's Professor Wiley tonight?" He was animated.

Wiley waved the smoke away from her face before making a move to leave. "Look, it's late. I have to be getting back to my apartment. I'll see you tomorrow morning in my office to go over the research we discussed," she said to Nina. Then she threw her overcoat around her shoulders and headed for the door.

"Boy, does she have a problem with me," Dewey blurted out. "Big deal, so I lit a cigarette. She smokes, too. I've seen her."

"You have not!" Nina said.

"Yes I have. Believe me."

"When?"

"Well, it's a secret," Dewey said, making his eyebrows dance. Then he leaned close and whispered, "I've taken her out a couple of times."

Nina stared at him with her mouth open. "No. No. You couldn't have. She wouldn't. Don't even try to..."

"I did. Several times," he whispered.

Nina put her hand on her cheek, mouth gaping, then composed herself. "So did she give you an A?"

"Actually, no. She gave me a B."

CHAPTER 5

Nina received an A on every final and faxed a copy of her grades to Wess Salinger at the Refugee Clinic in Miami. Along with her grades, she included a letter of recommendation from Professor Wiley.

On the night before she was to leave for Miami, Anthony called Nina down from her room to tell her that a package had been delivered for Remmy and could she pick it up for her. Nina walked downstairs to receive it. The return address was Professor Lynn Wiley. "Who delivered this?"

Nina shook it up and down, then put her ear to it.

"I don't know who she was. But boy was she fine. She really wanted to see Remmy, but I told her, Remmy had not been here in over a week. She looked real confused."

Nina laughed and sat down on Anthony's desk, playing with her long hair.

"So where has Ms. Remmy gone to now?" Anthony asked.

"She and Nicholas went to the Florida Keys."

"How is that girl ever going to pass law school?"

"Oh, she's a brain," Nina said with an incriminating grin, walking backwards down the hall with the package under her arm.

When she reached the room, she opened the package and found a card on top of some bubble wrap. The card said:

Dear Remmy,

Here is a little present to send you off to the Refugee Clinic. I am proud to know a young woman with such noble pursuits. I know you will do a wonderful job.

Professor Wiley

Nina dug her hand underneath the bubble wrap. She could not help but squeeze a couple of the bubbles to control her nerves. Then her hand fell upon something small, something hard...she pulled it out. It was a new tape recorder.

The first day in Miami was a balmy, December morning. It was the kind of morning where Nina liked to sip coffee outside and watch the people walk along South Beach. She gave half of her bagel to a homeless man, then headed for the Refugee Clinic.

"May I help you?" the receptionist asked.

"Yes, I'm Remmy Peterson. I'm a law student at NYU. I'm here to help Mr. Salinger with asylum claims."

"Is he expecting you?" She looked down at her appointment book.

"Oh, of course."

The receptionist walked to the back of the clinic to summon Mr. Salinger as Nina found a chair in the waiting room. It was a crowded lobby with many young people and children waiting to meet with an attorney. Nina listened to a little girl sing a song that she recognized in the Creole language, bringing memories back of her time in Haiti. She smiled at Nina and drew her a picture with the receptionist's pen on the back of a napkin. The picture had a house and some trees with a stick family in front of it.

"Merci," Nina said, smiling graciously and folding the napkin into the pocket of her suit jacket.

"Ms. Peterson, I thought I told you I do not accept first year students in my program." His voice was stern and his hands on his hips. The little girl jumped into Nina's lap and threw her arms around her as if for protection.

"Did you not get my FAX?"

"FAX?"

Nina kissed the little girl on the head between her braids, set her down and briskly walked past Mr. Salinger until she found the office with the fax machine. She picked up a heap of papers in the receiving pile and rummaged through them until she found the copy of her grades and Wiley's recommendation. She held it up in the air, waving it.

He grabbed it out of her hand and put on his reading glasses.

"Ms. Peterson, welcome. Can I get you some coffee or something to drink?" said the receptionist at the Detention Center after examining Nina's clearance badge.

"I would love some coffee."

"Would you..."

"I like it black, thank you."

The receptionist gave Nina some coffee, then walked her to a private room with a glass window that had a chair behind it.

"Will you be needing a translator? Mr. Salinger didn't say that you needed one."

"Yes, that's because my client speaks English."

When Nina was alone, she pulled a chair up to the window to wait for Amandine. Nina knew that she looked like a different person in her disguise, yet she was certain that if anyone would recognize her it would be Amandine.

"Now who might you be?" asked Amandine from behind the window. She was wearing an orange jumper given to her by the Detention Center and looked frail and tired.

Nina ran to the window and put her hand up to it as if to touch her friend. "Oh, Amandine, it's so wonderful to see you. But it hurts me to see you this way."

Amandine rolled her eyes. "Please. Save your sympathy act for someone else. I don't need you." She had her arms folded across her chest.

"But why? You're going to be deported. I need to help you with your case."

"Sorry. I'm not talking to some hot shot who's looking to build her resume. I am waiting for Nina. She is the only one I trust."

Nina leaned closed to the glass and spoke in a quiet voice. "Amandine, can anyone hear our conversation in here?"

"I do not know. But I would not be surprised. Why?"

Nina tipped the front of her wig and displayed a strand of her blonde hair.

"What? What are you doing? This is bizarre. I am going back to my cell," she said. "Guard?"

"No. No wait."

Amandine turned around.

Nina removed her large, cumbersome glasses and pressed her face up to the glass.

Amandine came towards her, outlining Nina's face with her finger. "It is one of the most beautiful faces I know. Nina, you have kept your promise. You have come for me."

As Nina did a formal interview with Amandine, she was able to fill in the gaps of what happened before and after the night the committee meeting was raided by the soldiers.

In 1990, Aristide was elected by the people in a democratic manner. Apparently Amandine's father, Arnaud Dubois, was a wealthy businessman and was for the new freedoms of the government. But there was a group that opposed the new way and some of the members threatened Amandine's father that he would lose his business and wealth if he did not support their cause. Frightened that they would form a coup and destroy him, he reluctantly cooperated with them, but made it clear to Blaise and Amandine that he was secretly an Aristide supporter.

Amandine and Blaise were not so clandestine. They were staunch Aristide supporters and were public about it until the coup in September of 1991. When the coup happened, Amandine's father told her that she should not come home until things settled down a bit. But then, in September 1992, he called to invite her for a short weekend because they were having a grand ball in their home and he told her to bring a friend. He promised her that they would be safe and made her promise that she would refrain from the secret meetings that were going on regarding Aristide and to stay secluded in the confines of his mansion and beach.

When the girls arrived, he had his bodyguards and chauffeur pick them up and take them straight to his home. The week they were there was splendid. They were waited on by Arnaud's staff and treated royally at the ball. If they had not ventured off the beach that day to go to the committee meeting, Amandine would have safely been on the plane that night with Nina and would have been back in NYU the next day.

After the girls fled from the meeting and hid in the secret compartment, the fisherman had taken them to people who were departing for the States in a wooden boat. Nina was taken back to the airport and Amandine began her journey at sea.

It had been arduous. She had been nauseated from the waves and became so dehydrated that she could barely cry tears. When she reached American soil about six days later, it was pitch black and cold, but they jumped in the water and swam to shore in their clothes. Then by foot they found their way to Ms. Raquel and Mr. Luc's rickety, white house by the beach. It was there that they hid in a back room and were fed rice and beans and plantains. Ms. Raquel had applied wet cloths on Amandine's head and wrists and fed her strong hot tea to bring her fever down.

When she was stronger in a few days, Luc helped her to get to the Refugee Clinic where she met with Wess Salinger about her case. There was a Haitian man there who was trying to get his status adjusted and he planned to take a bus to New York City to meet his brother the next day. He spoke to Amandine and agreed to find Nina when he arrived in the city to let her know that Amandine made it to America. Apparently, he had followed Nina from Hayden Hall to Hugos and made various attempts to talk to her alone, but it was only when she was tap-dancing on the table that he could get her attention and that is when he slipped Nina the note. His name was Pierre and he was worried about his own status and did not wish to be caught by anyone aiding another refugee. When he had returned to Miami for his hearings, he had stopped by the white house to find Amandine and gave her some money to call Nina on a public phone at a nearby coffee shop. It was there that he bought her some strong coffee and they got to talk about their dreams. After that, he would come by the white house after work. He was a door guard at one of the fancy apartment houses near South Beach. His visits are what kept Amandine going each day, and he still visited her each morning at the Detention Center.

Nina worked in the back room of the Refugee Clinic on an oblong table with other law students. She had access to a personal computer and research and used these tools to prepare an asylum claim for Amandine. First item on the agenda was to get her paroled.

Every so often, Wess Salinger would come in to oversee the students work and make comments. He did all his own secretarial work and besides the receptionist, was the only paid employee.

He sat next to Nina and answered her questions methodically, yet underneath his legalistic jargon, was a twinkle of passion in his eyes for what he was doing. At night, he took the law students out for drinks at South Beach. They did Salsa dancing and discussed their cases. They came from all over America, eager students, spending their Christmas vacation helping refugees.

In the day, they would lunch at the various restaurants in Little Haiti dining on rice and beans and fried plantains. At the end of the week, she submitted her work to Wess.

"Excellent, Remmy. It will be filed in the morning."

She spent Christmas with her mother in Delray Beach. Natasia lived in a condo and Nina slept on her couch. On New Years Eve, they went to Beachers, a popular restaurant and bar on Delray Beach. They had live Reggae music and Natasia won the limbo contest.

The last week of winter break, Nina spent everyday with her mother in the condo clubhouse playing canasta. Nina learned how to play well and charmed the elderly residents.

"It's a good thing she's going to law school next year," Natasia's dance student pronounced one night at the clubhouse. "Good looks only go so far."

"Speak for yourself, Ziv." Natasia flipped her hair flirtatiously at him.

As Nina watched her mother, she thought back to a time in Moscow when she was little and had been sitting in the kitchen while Natasia was cooking. Natasia had leaned over with a wooden spoon filled with some cabbage soup and Nina had teased her tongue with it. It had tasted nice. Then Natasia had moved over to Nina's father, offering him a taste. He sucked it with his lips then gave Natasia a kiss on her forehead, complimenting her as the greatest cook and she had flipped her hair at him in the same way she had just done to Ziv.

Nina smiled at her mother, observing how pretty she was. Nina had learned all her moves from watching her. Natasia walked with the grace of a dancer and could mesmerize anyone with her eyes.

Nina's father had always wanted to come over to the States and now with the new freedoms in Russia, Nina hoped he could obtain the proper papers with Nina, of course, conducting the legal work.

The last night in Delray, there was a knock on Natasia's door.

"Surprise." It was Remmy. She and Nicholas had made their way North with a rent-a-car from the Florida Keys. Nina had told them she would be there.

"Come in. Come in." Natasia waved and sat them down for some stew she was cooking.

"This is incredible," Nicholas said, patting his mouth with a red cloth napkin.

"Oh, I have all kinds of recipes."

"I'd love to try all of them." He winked and Remmy smacked him on the elbow.

"So where are you off to next?" Natasia asked.

"Vegas. We're gonna get married," Remmy said.

Nina spit her drink out of her mouth.

"Nini, what is this?" Natasia cringed. "Forgive her, please." She walked over with a cloth and handed it to Nina.

Nina wiped her mouth. "This can't be." She looked at Nicholas.

He bit his nails. "It's her idea," he said quietly. "She wants to be married by an Elvis impersonator on Las Vegas Blvd."

"You've flipped. Your parents will never forgive you."

"They don't need to know," she said. "I'm keeping my name."

"I'm keeping it, too, actually." Nina flashed her a conspiratorial smile. "Come with me." She waved for Remmy to follow her and they walked out onto the screen porch.

"I aced all your exams so you'll be good to transfer to any law school you want next year. But for now, I need to still be you until Amandine's claim is granted. Her hearing is next August."

"Fine with me," she said. "But I'm not transferring. I'm withdrawing when you're ready."

"What about your parents?"

"I don't care. Nicholas is going to get his Doctorate and become a professor. We could live comfortably."

"Remmy, you have no idea how to live just comfortably."

"I'll learn."

"It's not so easy to go backwards."

"Your friend Amandine did."

"Not by choice." Her face was drawn.

83

"How's she holding up?"

"Okay, I guess. She has this guy who comes to visit her every day. Keeps her up."

"How romantic. Maybe they can get married and she can become a citizen."

"I thought of that. But he's not a citizen yet, either."

"Do you think you can win your case?"

"It's a long shot, but I'm going to give it everything I have."

"You're remarkable. I don't know anyone else who would risk this much for a friend, except like Robin Hood." She howled.

"Well, I was a refugee myself, don't forget. I know how it feels."

"I don't know how anything is supposed to feel, but I think I'm in love." She moved close to Nina and whispered, "Nina, I respect you and your opinion. Why don't you like Nicholas?"

"I love Nicholas. He's one of my closest friends, but I don't think he's ready to get married. He's still finding himself."

"Aren't we all?"

"I suppose. But I don't think Nicholas is ready to settle down with, with one woman, just yet."

Remmy covered her hands with her eyes. "I don't know what to do."

"Just take it slow." She held Remmy's arm and led her back to the condo.

In January of 1993, Nina started her second semester of law school as Remmy Peterson. Meanwhile, she scheduled her acting classes around the law ones, she needed six more theater credits to graduate.

Nina waded through the first day of Criminal Procedure and Legal Process, noticing that Marcy Weiner, the girl that had been drenched in water, had sat near Nina in both of her morning classes.

Marcy had discarded the big bow that had once seemed stapled to her head and had her hair cut in a conservative bob.

"How was your Christmas break?" Nina asked.

"It was okay. How was Haiti?"

"Um, Little Haiti," Nina corrected. "It was an interesting place with beautiful people. My work was very rewarding."

"Awesome, maybe I'll come with you next time." She gave a conciliatory smile. "Hey, do you want to get some lunch?"

"Really?"

"Yes, really."

After Nina and Marcy shared a long lunch in a café in the Village, they went to the bookstore to buy books for the new semester and agreed to share the cost of a couple of textbooks.

"I never thought I'd be sharing a book with you." Marcy joked.

"Hey, I'm sorry about the water."

"It was a clever presentation. I wish I would have thought of it."

"Thanks."

Later, as Nina was studying, there was a knock at the door.

"Who is it?"

"Nina, it's Anthony. There's an important call for Remmy. Where is that girl?"

Nina opened the door. "Come in."

"Oh no. I've got to get back downstairs." He peeked around the room. "It's a sure nice room you got here."

"Oh, it's not my stuff. Remmy thinks a dorm room is supposed to be in a Martha Stewart catalogue." They laughed, "So who's on the phone?"

"Some guy named Wess."

"Ah, I know him." She scratched her head. "I'll talk to him, tell him Remmy's in Vegas."

Nina raced to the phone booth and shut the glass door, making sure Anthony had gone back to his station.

"Remmy Peterson here."

"Parole granted."

Nina's heart soared. "That's so wonderful. Thank you."

"No, thank you."

"So where is she?"

"Well, she's still in the Detention Center. We need to have a legitimate place for her to stay, preferably with an American citizen who lives nearby."

"Why can't she just stay with Pierre?"

"Oh that's not a good idea. The INS may think they are planning a fraud marriage for immigration purposes. She needs to show she's in a stable environment, and not milking the system. It becomes an economic issue. Americans don't want immigrants taking their tax money from the welfare system."

"They forget their ancestors were once immigrants."

"Each and every one of them were immigrants, unless they're Native Americans, of course."

"I have an idea. I know a lady who was once a refugee herself. She lives in a condo in Delray. She might be interested in a roomy."

"You have all kinds of tricks up your sleeve."

"You have no idea." She laughed cunningly, twirling her hair. "Look Wess, I have a favor to ask you. Can I do an internship there this summer so that I can help prepare for Amandine's case?"

"Remmy, I'd love to have you and you are more than welcome, but I can't pay you."

"I get loans to pay for school, all I need is spending money."

"Sorry, we don't have the resources," he said softly. "But, hey, you're a big wig A student, you can get a job in a fancy firm."

"Who wants it?"

"It might be good. You can use all of their resources and library, and work on her case on your own time. Who knows? Maybe you can even get an attorney there to volunteer time to work on the case. We could sure use the help. Maybe try Peterson & Peterson. Any relation?"

"Uh, no." She cleared her throat. "I heard McNamara & Associates has a much better immigration department."

McNamara & Associates was not just the largest law firm in the city, but it was one of the most recognized firms in the world. Therefore, issues important to big commercial giants like fortune five hundred companies were of highest priority in determining where the firm should concentrate its practice. However, because the firm had such a famous profile, occasionally they represented international figures and good will cases that kept them well-esteemed with notoriety in the international community. Jim McNamara's father, Martin McNamara, was still in control of the firm, yet spent most of his days on the golf course. He was largely a figurehead and made speeches and talked to the press, but it was Jim McNamara who oversaw the day to day activities.

Nina graduated from NYU with a Theater major in May and then while her peers were auditioning for theatrical parts around the city, she was spending the summer acting as Remmy Peterson. She spent the first few weeks of her internship at McNamara & Associates assisting attorneys in the immigration department as she had requested. However, she learned very fast that these immigration cases were mostly shuffling papers for international sports figures and the like. Among the pending cases, as far as Nina could see, was not one political asylum claim.

When Nina had first arrived at the firm she was greeted with the most sincere accolades for her achievements at New York University.

"Well, I can't tell you how excited we all are to have you here," Yvonne Lindell-Frank had said, clearly not recognizing Nina in her Remmy disguise. "We know you are one of the brightest students in your class. And we are especially honored that you passed up your grandfather's firm over at Peterson so that you could be on our team."

Nina almost choked on her black coffee. She had not thought that the attorneys at McNamara would know about Remmy's connection, New York being such a large city. But she soon found that was not the case. It was a big deal for McNamara to get a Peterson and he was going to give her the royal treatment.

Yvonne Lindell-Frank marched Nina around the office introducing her to several attorneys. She shook their hands and memorized their names.

"Most of our interns work in cubicles or in the library. But because you're our most sought after intern, Mr. McNamara insisted that you have your own office," Lindell-Frank explained.

"You're going to like it," a small man said with a leap and a clap. "It has a window."

They spun Nina around and all marched her towards her office. Nina's mouth opened and her eyes were wide. It was bigger than Lindell-Frank's office. It had a panoramic window, a mahogany desk and credenza, a cushioned chair, a telephone and a personal computer.

"Your secretary, Cherie, will give you all the supplies you need."

"My secretary?"

"That's right." Yvonne walked out of the room, into the doorway. "Well, I'll be leaving you now. Mr. McNamara is going to want you to attend case review in a couple of weeks, where we go over cases and ideas. It will be your job to assist the immigration attorneys, at your request. You must get us up to speed at the meeting."

"I'll be ready."

"So mother, how are you and Amandine getting along?"

"Like sisters. She is the best dancer in my class, does the tango better than Ziv."

"She goes to classes with you?"

"Of course. And afterward we get a cappuccino. And on Fridays, we have our nails done."

"Unbelievable. I'm working like a dog and everyone else is having a party."

"You can join us whenever you like," Natasia said. "Guess who else is staying with us?"

"Who?"

"Your friend Remmy." She had a bubbly laughter. "After five months in Las Vegas, she maxed out her credit cards and she could not use her father's cards because he would trace them back to Las Vegas and she is supposed to be in New York or something like that."

"And what about Nicholas?"

"Oh you will not believe. He did not show up for their wedding."

"I'm not surprised."

"Well, she is better for it. We are having a ball."

"Why did she come to see you?"

"She thought you would be here."

Nina rolled her eyes. "I told her I was working in New York. So how are they supporting themselves? Are you paying for them?"

"Oh no, I don't have that kind of money. Ziv got them a job waiting tables at the bagel shop."

"Amandine and Remmy?" Nina hooted. "Now that's a sight to see."

A few weeks later, Nina had prepared all her cases and was ready for case review. As she was standing in the hall outside the conference room, she was introduced to several attorneys and shook hands in an obligatory manner.

"And I imagine you know this guy?" McNamara said, his hand on the shoulder of a handsome, familiar face.

Nina took deep breaths through her nose, then flung her arms around Steve Peterson, Remmy's brother, and gave him a kiss on the cheek. "It's so wonderful to see you here."

Steve stepped back, his eyebrow raised, looking perplexed as McNamara pushed him along to meet other attorneys. As he was doing his perfunctory duty, he kept looking back at Nina, shrugging, but she tried to ignore him.

Once inside the conference room, they took their places around a long table with McNamara at the head. A secretary poured them each a glass of water with lemon slices. They took turns, going around the room, discussing cases such as anti-trust and contracts. When it was Steve's turn, he explained that he decided to leave his grandfather's firm and start his own solo practice. What he was asking from McNamara & Associates was the opportunity to use their facilities and resources.

"Will you be needing office space?"

"No. I plan to get my own space in a few months, but perhaps I could just use your library."

"Wouldn't you know it, the grandson of the owner of our rival firm wants to use our library. What's wrong with granddaddy's library?" McNamara and friends were humored.

"Well, as you must know, they are not very happy with my decision to leave their firm."

"Oh, well we are very happy. How about working for us?"

He blushed. "Oh, that's very kind of you. But I have always dreamed of working for myself."

McNamara nodded, though somewhat disapproving. "What do you think?" He looked at Nina. "Should we let him?"

Nina sat up in her chair, blushing too, as all eyes were on her. "Of course."

When it was Nina's turn to go over her cases she did in a thorough, articulate manner that was greeted with approval.

"Fine work," McNamara said. "Do you have any questions about the firm or anything we do?"

"Um, just one." She straightened up in her chair with ample posture. "Do we have any political asylum cases pending?"

McNamara waved his index finger in the air. "You know, that's an interesting question. I can't recall such a case." He looked around the room for feedback. "No seriously, the work of undocumented immigrants is usually for bleeding hearts." McNamara pointed to an attorney that was sitting next to Nina. "Hey Bernard, how would you like to become our first bleeding heart?"

Bernard flashed a wide grin. "Ha, do I still get to have a fancy paycheck?"

As the attorneys snickered, McNamara clapped his hands and said, "Why you can have any style of paycheck you want as long as I'm not footing the bill."

Nina banged her hand on the table interrupting their party. "Excuse me, but I don't think this is funny."

Laughter ceased and everyone stared at Nina. McNamara cleared his throat. "I'm sorry. We just like to have fun." He folded his arms across his chest and became serious. "So was there a reason for your question?"

"Um, yes. I interviewed a woman yesterday who claims to be the daughter of an important businessman in Haiti. She went against the politics of the country and was chased by the military. She had to flee her country on a wooden boat to escape persecution. She made it to Florida, but was eventually picked up by the INS. She's on parole waiting for her asylum hearing."

"I think I heard something like that story before. What was her name?" Lindell-Frank asked.

"Amandine Dubois."

"No. I thought it was a Nina something."

"Um, Nina is not generally a Haitian name," Nina said. She heard Steve chuckle quietly.

"Oh that's right. Come to think of it, Nina was the woman who told me about the case. She was a friend or something. Claimed to have been over there too. She said something about a camera hidden inside a secret compartment. She wanted us to play spy and go over and get it." Yvonne said.

Everyone laughed.

"Well, why don't you? Amandine said the pictures have great evidence of her case."

"This is absurd," McNamara interrupted. "Now let's get back to more important matters. Who has a case they want to discuss?"

Nina walked back to Hayden Hall where she still resided in her dorm for the summer. Every night, she lay awake in her small, narrow bed, plotting her case. She knew that without any evidence, Amandine would only have her testimony in claiming to be persecuted for political reasons. It was true that asylum could be granted on testimony, but if she could get the camera, it would be stronger. She could develop pictures and show Amandine's house and family before she fled to America. She could find the people in the photographs to maybe serve as witnesses, then she could show Amandine at the committee meeting, and finally pictures of the raid. It would be better.

At dawn, she would wake up and do her other assignments so she would have time during the day to do research in the library on Federal procedures in Amandine's case. Each morning around 4:30 a.m., Nina typed research notes and briefs for other attorneys in a frenzy, pulling out the paper, manually, as she reached the bottom of the page. Then she put the notes in the correct files in her cabinet so she could not commingle her research.

Afterwards, Nina would review some of her files, then examined some treatises and law review articles for clarification. At around 6:00, she would take a shower, have two cups of black coffee and dress in an oversized suit. She was typically in the library by 7:00 a.m., pondering recent case law while her colleagues would roll in between 8:00 and 9:00 a.m.

One morning around 7:30 a.m., Nina was beside a file of federal case law reviewing some decisions on political asylum when she heard shuffling near the coffee maker. It sounded as if someone was using an espresso machine. Nina was nervous because the office was usually quiet in the early morning. Nina was always the caretaker at this time arousing the sleepy heads with her shots of double black coffee as they entered the workplace. Now someone had intruded into her domain. Nina poked her head into the coffee room. She saw a man's hand pouring white foam into a porcelain cup. It looked just like Remmy's teacup, the one that had been shattered across their dorm room floor. Nina compared her own drinking vessel. It was a Styrofoam cup that was chewed around the rim. She moved closer and saw the back of his head. It had brown curls. He twisted to the side to add sugar. Nina grimaced. She hated sweet coffee. But she noticed that the man had a handsome profile outlined by a prominent, square jaw. Nina squinted her eyes to focus. Yes, once again, it was Steve Peterson.

Nina backed out of the room before he could see her. She was completely nervous about him questioning her about their last encounter and still humiliated about when she had been naked in his bathroom in Connecticut, but he obviously did not know she was the same girl. Nina slipped back into the library, but Steve walked in shortly after. She pretended to read cases and ignore him. He sat next to her trying hard to make eye contact, but she never looked his way. Then she ran to her office.

She immediately called Remmy at her mother's house. The phone rang twelve times.

"Hello," said a hoarse voice.

"Hi! Is this Remmy?"

"Yes. Who is this?"

"It's Nina."

"What on earth are you doing up at this hour?"

"Oh, please. I've been up for three hours."

Remmy was coughing into the phone. "You haven't called me in forever, and now you call at some crazy hour." More groans.

"Look, I'll let you get back to sleep in a minute. I have to get to work. But please, tell me what am I supposed to say to your brother?"

"My brother, you saw him?" Remmy sounded more alert. "I can't believe this. Steve ditched my grandfather's law firm."

"Why?"

"I don't know. He got this, like, idealistic bug that he wanted to help society and be his own boss. You remember how he acted when you were at my house?"

Nina laughed. She could still see Harold jiggling his ice in his Scotch glass and Steve escaping into the kitchen.

"Oh, your grandfather must be distraught."

"You have no idea. I don't care though, it makes me look good." She had a hoarse chuckle. "I'm kidding of course. Hello?"

"Look, I'm going to try to avoid your brother. I don't want anyone in this office finding out that I'm not Remmy Peterson."

"This is getting hairy. If Steve questions you, just tell him you are another girl named Remmy Peterson."

"Do you think he'll buy it?"

"We can only hope."

Nina spent the next couple of days laboriously hiking the back staircase and dodging behind cubicles to avoid Steve. As soon as she would spot his shiny shoes, she would become feverish.

"Gotta go!" She yelled at McNamara abruptly when she saw Steve approaching on his fifth day of working in the library at McNamara & Associates. She quickly retreated to the back staircase and hung onto the railing as she skipped a couple of steps. She ran down almost tripping over her heels, when suddenly she heard a door slam from above. She could feel her pulse throbbing as she ran faster, then she stumbled on her heels and fell down several steps. She landed with her skirt hiked up, exposing her thighs. She immediately retrieved her glasses and put them on.

"Are you all right?" Steve extended his hand to help her up. She looked into his face and had trouble avoiding his eyes.

"I'm fine. I'm fine," she said as he helped her into a standing position.

She dusted off her skirt and turned away on her toes. "Well, thank you. I better get going." She began to totter away with a little limp.

"Wait a minute!" Steve yelled after her. "Who are you? And how do you know me?"

"I don't. I was just pretending." She kept moving.

"Why?"

"Because, because they thought I knew you and so, I didn't want to disappoint them."

"Oh, I see. That's why you gave me a big smooch on the cheek. Not that I minded of course, at least you don't wear lipstick."

"Excuse me, but I have to go."

"Wait, you can at least tell me your name."

Nina turned to him. "You don't know, you don't know my name?"

"No, McNamara didn't tell me because he thought I knew you already and you being a crowd-pleaser, gave me a kiss. But I don't much buy that, because you didn't care much about pleasing the crowd when you brought up your political asylum pitch."

"Well, that's very important to me."

"I see." He smiled, displaying perfect white teeth. "Can I buy you lunch?"

"Lunch?"

Nina sat in an elegant café in Greenwich Village next to a man who had already seen her completely naked.

He drank some French wine and Nina had cranberry juice with vodka. Then he sliced some crepes and put some onto Nina's plate.

"So are you ever going to tell me your name?" Steve asked.

"Name, yes, I could tell you that, sure, I'm Madelline."

"Madelline..."

"Madelline Croft." She extended her hand and he took it in his.

"Pleased to meet you Ms. Croft."

"Likewise." She nibbled some food and turned the conversation to him. "So why did you leave your family's firm?"

He looked down at his crepes and pushed them around with his fork. "I love my family. I really do. But I just have trouble working for them. I mean it's all about billing hours. I'm just looking for something with some more substance." As he sipped his wine, Nina admired his strong hands.

"I want to work for something I believe in," he said. "I want to, you know, make a difference."

Nina smiled in agreement. "I know what you mean. There are so many people in law school who actually hate the law, but they stay there anyway because they think they're going to make a fortune." She thought of Joseph Dewey and the young women dancing with the books on their heads.

"That's sad. It's not money that makes people happy."

"That's true," Nina said. "We were really poor when I was growing up. But my mother and I had so much fun together. We used to spend hours together, making clothes we couldn't afford to buy." Nina smiled, nostalgically. "She wanted me to go to school looking pretty."

"What a wonderful relationship."

"Oh, it's the best. But my mother, she had her priorities in order. We may not have had our electric bill paid, but she never left our apartment without looking like a million bucks." Nina nibbled on her crepes.

"What about your father?"

"My father?" She pulled a picture of him from her briefcase, then handed it to Steve. "That's him, eating breakfast before he goes off to work." She pointed to her father. He was sitting at the table in a tiny kitchen. "That's in Moscow." She put her hand on her mouth, wishing she hadn't revealed so much.

Steve examined her. "You're Russian?"

She nodded and looked at her plate.

He sipped some wine. "Your name, Madelline Croft, it's not a bit Russian."

"What's in a name?" she tried, but he continued to scrutinize her, so she cleared her throat and said, "my mother changed our name. We thought it would be easier, to um, assimilate."

"So you were born in Russia?"

Nina nodded, wishing she could disappear.

"When did you come here?"

"My mother and I left Russia when I was six. We never went back."

"Wow! Do you remember it at all?"

"Just little things, like, my father coming home at night, singing and kind of throwing me up in the air, giving me kisses." Her chin sank into her chest. "I used to wait by the door for him to come home," she added, her voice constricted.

Steve patted her hand. "Maybe you'll see him again some day."

"I hope so." Nina smiled, dreamily. "But it would be so strange. I wouldn't know what to say."

He leaned in close to her. "I'm sure he'll be amazed at how successful you turned out."

Nina blushed. "Thank you. So what cases are you working on? Anything interesting?"

Steve sat back in his chair, clearing his throat. "Oh, nothing really yet. I'm just sort of getting acclimated. But I'm looking for something to work on. Maybe I can help you with that political asylum claim."

Nina's blood started pumping and her hands trembled. She heard herself speak, before she could think. "Great. We could really use the help."

"I'm looking forward to it." His eyes were animated. "Hey, I have a question. Do you know my sister Remmy? She was in your class at NYU and works at McNamara."

"Oh yes, um, of course."

"Well, I don't know what she's up to. I keep stopping by her office and leaving notes, but I can't seem to get in touch with her. Maybe she's avoiding me because I left the family firm."

"She left, too."

"Yes, but that is only temporary. She told my dad that she was only working at McNamara this summer to learn their secrets."

"She didn't."

"Oh yes, she did. She's a serious student. All A's."

"Is that right?"

"As far as I'm concerned she can take over the whole Peterson firm. I'd be happy for her. You can tell her that if you see her."

"I'll be sure to remember."

CHAPTER 6

The next morning, Nina didn't go to work at 7:00 a.m.; instead, she went to the Village Coffee Shop. She had not been there since Nicholas and Randy left. She had no idea where Nicholas had gone to after Las Vegas, but over the past year, Randy trained to be an immigration officer. The story she told him last September inspired him to want to help process papers for immigrants coming into the country, though he admitted, often he had to deny papers and that part of the job he did not like.

Instead of her usual stool at the counter where she used to chat with Randy, she opted for a secluded booth back in the corner in Randy's old station. She studied the menu, deciding it was exactly the same as last year and probably the last fifty years.

Although it was morning, she ordered a BLT.

She ordered Randy a chocolate milk shake and two eggs over easy with white toast. She remembered that he used to love to soak his whole pieces of bread in the eggs and swirl them around his plate. This would be the first time she would see Randy since before Christmas break.

He came into the restaurant about fifteen minutes late, sporting a uniform. His midriff had been flattened and his muscles were now defined.

She waved at him, but he did not respond, so she stood up and walked over to him, then took off her wig.

"Nina?"

She smiled, coyly.

"What? Did you get some cool part in a play? I thought you were going to law school next fall."

"I am. And this is my new look."

"Nice. I guess."

"Look, law school is not a fashion contest. I need to be serious."

"Whatever makes you happy."

She gave him a hug, then they found their way to the table Nina reserved.

"Randy, I'm sorry I haven't kept in touch lately. I've been swamped with studies." She cleared her throat. "But now I had some time so I needed to see you. I need to ask you for a favor."

Randy nodded his head as he stared at Nina straight in the eyes. "You know I would always help you."

She eyed him curiously.

"Of course, it would have to be legal. I work for the government, you know."

"And you like it?"

"I love it. But it can get real emotional sometimes."

"Well, you look fantastic. I'm so proud of you."

He smiled demurely. "So? What is it? What does Nina need?"

"I'm stalling because you said the favor I ask you has to be legal."

"And...it's not?"

"It's not illegal, but let's just say, it could make people suspicious."

Randy scratched his head and sipped some ice water. "No wonder Nicholas used to call you the little Russian spy."

Nina chuckled. "How is Nicholas?"

"Nicholas is Nicholas." There was more laughter. "He's in L.A. trying to get his screenplay sold, then in the fall he's coming back here to get his Doctorate."

"What happened with Remmy?"

"Remmy? That's old news. They split up the day of their wedding."

"Why?"

"You know Nicholas. He just wasn't ready. And personally, I don't think Remmy was either."

The food Nina had ordered arrived and she could tell Randy was disappointed. He nibbled on his toast and ordered herbal tea.

"I'm sorry," Nina said, "I thought you liked..."

"No, it's fine, really. Look. I hope you're not annoyed, but I have to leave here in ten minutes so you better tell me about your favor." Randy was whispering.

"Remember that night I told you about what happened to me in Haiti?"

"Yeah, of course I do. It's why I work in immigration."

"Well, do you remember when I told you I left a camera there with important photographs inside the wall of a cottage?"

"Yeah, I remember something about a camera."

"Well I'm going back to Haiti to get it."

"You can't do that."

"I already have the paper work to get into the country because I was there last September, but it needs to be updated. Can you do that for me?"

Randy thought for a moment, then looked back at Nina. "Sure. I can do that. I can do that for you."

Nina smiled at him and thanked him under her breath.

"Hey, don't you think it's too dangerous to go over there?"

"No. I'm not worried about it. I'm just going for one night and I'm going with an attorney. He's agreed to take Amandine's case."

"It's a he, huh?" He winked, then stood up to leave. "So is that all? Is there anything else I can do for you, counselor?"

"Well, there is one more thing."

"Of course," he said.

106

"I'm going to need a new picture on my passport; one that looks like I do now with red hair and glasses."

Randy scratched his temple with his index finger, now deeply engrossed in what she was saying.

Nina continued. "I'm wondering if you could manage that for me."

Randy paused for several moments, absorbing the information. Then he finally said, "Very interesting. You're wanting me to help you officially change your identity." Randy scrutinized Nina's face. "You really are like a Russian spy, aren't you?" He leaned his face close to hers as though they might be kissing if they were any closer.

Nina's face was tight. She was blinking excessively, waiting for an answer. "Look, forget it. I'll go down there and get a picture done myself. There's nothing illegal about changing your looks."

"No, but when someone is traveling into a country with political problems for one night and they want a complete identity change, there may be a bit of questioning about what you're trying to accomplish."

"Well, that's why I came to you."

"Look, like you said, there's nothing illegal about it. I'm just curious that's all. But I'm on it. I'm doing the papers today."

"Really? You'd do that for me?"

"Of course. Come down to my office this afternoon to get your picture taken and I'll have your papers ready for you in the morning."

"Thanks." She gave him a firm hug. Then together, they left the coffee shop.

Washington Square Park was a source of perpetual motion and continuing entertainment for neighbors whose dwellings skimmed the outskirts. Nina sat on a bench near the fountain after work remembering the carefree times she had with Amandine and Randy and Nicholas, singing and dancing in the park. They spent many nights getting pizza and staying up all night smoking cigarettes and discussing their philosophies about life.

Now she sat on the bench in a disguise looking for Randy to pop around the fountain in his INS uniform with her traveling papers. He had called her earlier and promised to deliver her passport to the park after work.

After an hour dragged by, Nina was nervous that Randy had changed his mind about helping her. Or even worse, had discovered that she was pretending to be Remmy and revealed her identity to everyone in law school and McNamara & Associates. But Randy did not know she was officially working at McNamara. He only knew that she and Steve were using McNamara's library.

When it began to get dark, she knew it was not safe to linger in the park any longer. She took off her wig then raided the vending machine at the dorm and sat down with Anthony for a dinner of candy bars.

That night she tossed in bed, feeling frightened with the notion that Randy had discovered her plan.

Nina lay in bed listening to every footstep that shuffled past her door. She could hear her mother's voice, "They are coming to take us back to Russia, Nina."

She jumped up in a cold sweat at 3:30 a.m., only an hour before her usual wake up time, took a shower and made her coffee extra strong. She thought about calling someone, Art in Connecticut; maybe she could tell him the whole story and he could help her. But then she did not want to drag Art into any trouble. The last she had spoken to him, he had done well in his senior year and was getting ready to start his first year of law school at Yale in Connecticut. Nina arrived at the office at 6:30 a.m., determined to beat Steve to the library and to see if there was any evidence that Randy had reported her intentions. She took off her shoes to avoid the loud sound of her heels from clicking against the floor. She poked her head into the library and twirled on her toes out the door when she saw Steve sitting on the table, swinging his feet with an envelope in his hand.

"Madelline!" he yelled as he ran after her down the hall. "What's wrong? I've been waiting for you."

Nina caught her breath. "Oh, it's you. Hi."

"Hi, that's all you could say?" He laughed in his charming way. "Why did you run out of the library when you saw me?"

"I don't know. Is everything okay? Did Randy tell you anything?"

"Randy? Who's Randy?"

Nina was quiet as she sat down on the floor.

Steve sat next to her. They had their backs to the wall near the water fountain. There was no one else in the office. "So why did you run away from me?"

"Run? I didn't run. I just was in a hurry to get to the bathroom. I, I have a rip in my pantyhose and I have to fix it."

"Let me see."

"What?"

"Let me see the rip."

"No I will not show you the rip."

He looked at her curiously.

"It's up here." Nina pointed to her inner thigh.

"Oh, I see."

Nina could feel her face get hot. She looked away from him.

"I'm sorry," Steve said, putting his hand on her shoulder. "I didn't mean to embarrass you."

"It's okay."

"But why do you have your shoes off? You're acting really strange."

Nina shrugged, then looked at the envelope in Steve's hand. "So what's that?" Nina asked.

"It's an envelope. I don't know what's in it. Some guy came by here last night looking for a Nina. He insisted that she was working on this case with me. I don't know what he's talking about, do you?"

Nina propped up. "Um yes. Nina Selinsky. She's the friend of Amandine who Yvonne Lindell-Frank was talking about. She was the one who was with Amandine when all of this happened in Haiti. Apparently, she really wants to be involved in this case." Nina extended her hands. "Here, I'll get this envelope to her."

"Well, he said he was supposed to deliver this envelope to Nina in the park, but that he couldn't make it. He said she told him I was working on the case with her and asked me to give her this envelope and when he handed it to me, he made me promise not to open it. He acted very suspiciously; kind of the way you're acting right now. What's going on?"

"Nothing. Nothing's going on." Nina grabbed the envelope from Steve and put it inside her suit jacket pocket.

"So what do you suggest we do now to get evidence on this case?"

"I think we need to go to Haiti and get that camera."

"You are crazy."

"Why?" Nina yelled. "If the photographs have the evidence on it that Amandine suggests, we could win her case for sure."

"Testimony may be all we need," Steve said.

"Maybe. But still, some physical evidence would be nice. We've got to prove that Amandine actually feared for her life when she fled Haiti and that this was based on political reasons. Testimony is good, but physical evidence would be even stronger."

Steve scratched his chin as he looked up at the ceiling. "We'll start off with Nina Selinsky. She was there. She'd be an excellent witness."

Nina gulped. "I don't know. I don't think she wants to be in the spotlight. She's afraid. She'd rather help, behind the scenes."

"Well I'm sorry that she's scared, but she really doesn't have anything to be afraid of. She's in America now and she's our key witness. If we have to, we'll subpoena her."

Nina chewed on her fingernail. "I could try to schedule an interview with her, but I don't think she'll show up."

"Why? Why wouldn't she show up? She wants to help Amandine. You just said so."

"I told you, she's afraid," Nina said like she was telling a secret.

Steve stared at Nina curiously. "Okay. If Nina doesn't show up, then we'll defer to your plan."

"Promise?"

"I promise."

The plane flight to Port-Au-Prince was not crowded, and they found a seat in the back. Steve was reading Dostoevsky and Nina was reading a legal treatise.

"Don't you ever stop studying law? It's better for your mind to not be so, one dimensional." Steve pulled the treatise from her face.

"You mean like a Jack of all trades, a master of nothing."

"It's better I think to taste all the fruits of life."

"It is only the masters who have great success."

"Depends on your meaning of success."

They had many conversations like this, comparing their philosophies, bantering about who was right.

"So why are you so interested in Russian writers?"

"I've always been interested in Russians." He winked.

She shrugged and went back to her treatise. The flight attendant brought them a drink. Steve had a beer and Nina had tomato juice.

"I always drink tomato juice in the air, but never on the ground." She took a sip, licking her lips so as not to have a red mustache.

"Any particular reason?"

"No."

They were served a small tray and Nina tried not to bump elbows with him as she cut her food.

"So now tell me, how did you know that Nina Selinsky wouldn't show up at my interview?"

Nina shrugged. "Female intuition." She was tired of lying. She wished she could just have a true conversation with him for just one day.

"I knew a Nina once, my sister's friend. She came to visit for dinner one night. Wow was she gorgeous."

Nina blushed, continuing to look down at her plate, cutting her food. "So did you ask her out?"

"Well no. I wanted to, but it was kind of awkward. She and my sister got in this bad fight and Nina locked herself in the bathroom. When I jimmied the door open, she was...," he put his hand up, "never mind."

"Come on, you shared this much."

"Well, all right. She was sitting there naked and man was she the most beautiful thing I've ever seen."

Nina rubbed her hands through her hair, trembling a little bit. "So are you going to let your affections be known?"

"You think I should?"

"Well, you obviously like her." Nina smiled, trying not to look incriminating.

"Well that's just the thing. I don't know her enough to like her. I just like the way she looks. I mean I fantasize about this woman."

Nina's heart was thumping and her face was flushed. She turned her face away, afraid to see his eyes. "I don't know if you should be telling me this."

He looked down. "Probably not. But there's something about you. You're so easy to talk to."

"Maybe Nina is too."

"Wouldn't that be a bonus?"

That afternoon, they arrived at the airport. Nina had to show her passport in a separate line so Steve would not see that the name on her papers was Nina Pavlova. When they were finished with customs, they were taken in a private car to an expensive resort known to cater to Americans and the employees spoke English.

"You are staying for just one night?" the concierge asked. "You will love it here and want to come back." He winked, then checked them in and led them to their room.

"I think he thought we were lovers," Steve said when the concierge left, chuckling.

"Well we do have one room." Nina sat on the bed and bounced up and down. "Firm. Just what I like. You can sleep on the couch."

"Can't we draw straws?" He chided, but then plopped on the sofa, propping up the pillows, crossing his feet. He wore brown leather shoes that still had a price tag on the bottom.

Nina came by and peeled it off. "Two hundred forty-eight dollars. If we get into trouble, we can sell them."

He chortled quietly, closing his eyes. "So now tell me, when did you become so passionate about helping refugees?"

She sat at the far end of the couch. "Well, I was a refugee," she said softly.

He sat up. "You told me you left Russia when you were six, but..."

"Yes. My mother was a ballerina who fled her troupe on a tour in New York. I was with her. She ran with me in her arms."

"Incredible. Where did you go?"

"We went out the back door through some narrow streets until we reached the subway. We kept riding back and forth. We were very lost. My mother spoke a little English. I spoke none."

"Was this planned?"

"No. It was rather serendipitous, so we had no plan and just kept riding the subway until someone led us to the office of this wonderful immigration attorney,

Soloman Horowitz. All of the work he did for his clients was from the love in his heart. He's my inspiration."

They rented bicycles and Steve trailed behind Nina along a street parallel to the beach. As they rode, Nina had flashbacks to the night she had fled with Amandine. It had been two times that she traveled that path; once with Amandine and the other with the fisherman when she headed back to the airport.

When they arrived at the wooden house by the beach, Theron was still on the porch, cleaning fish with a metal tool. Nina knew he would not recognize her in her disguise. She was wearing an oversized dress and straw hat, and a backpack with their travel papers. However, she hoped he would help them.

They dragged their bicycles up on the sand, and lay them down before going up the steps. Nina led the way.

"Hello," she said, smiling, but the man did not respond kindly. Instead, he was stammering in Creole, using large hand gestures to indicate that they should go away. When they did not move, he chased them off the porch with a stick in hand. They ran to the back, Steve holding Nina's hand. In the back, they crouched down, taking short breaths.

"Now what?"

"I thought this might happen," Nina said. "I have an idea. You stay here."

"What? You're going back there by yourself? No way."

"Trust me. I know what I'm doing." She stood up. "I'll be right back." She glanced over at him, admiring him in his more casual look, white tennis shoes and Bermudas, crouching behind the house, preciously vulnerable.

When Nina was away from Steve's eyesight, she inched her way to the front of the house, then up to the porch and dared to sit beside Theron. She pulled her hat, glasses and wig off and stuffed them in her pack as she let her long hair fall down her back.

He looked astonished with his mouth opened. "Nina?"

She nodded.

"Amandine?"

"Bon." She used the French word for good, making him smile.

He led her into the cottage and opened the trap door. To her amazement, Arnaud and Blaise were sitting there on the floor, eating out of clay bowls with their fingers. The last time she had seen Arnaud, he was sitting in his mansion at the dining table, being waited on by servants.

"Nina." Blaise jumped to his feet, embracing her.

"Where is my Amandine?" said Arnaud.

Nina crouched down next to him. He was searching her eyes for hope. "Is my daughter okay?"

"She is well." Nina smiled triumphantly. "She is living with my mother in Florida."

Tears came to his eyes and he wiped them with the back of his hand. "That is so wonderful. Thank you."

"So what are you doing here?" Blaise asked.

"Well Amandine is only on parole right now. We must prove that she has a real fear of persecution in order for her to be granted asylum."

"That should not be difficult." Arnaud's voice was deep.

"Well, you wouldn't think so, but asylum claims can be complicated," she explained. "That's why I'm here. I left the camera in here the night Amandine fled because I thought we might be followed. I came now to get it." She reached up on a wooden ledge, sweeping her hand and placing the dusty camera into her palm.

Blaise touched it. "Yes, I remember this. I took many pictures with that camera. You must get it to a safe place and get it developed." His expression was grave. "But make sure you take out the lovely pictures of you and Amandine on the beach."

"You took pictures of us with this camera?"

"Yes, so that you would have it for a good memory. I did not anticipate all these problems."

"So there are pictures of me on this camera?"

"Oh, yes."

"This isn't good. Steve will know it's me. The real me." She tapped her fingers on her leg, thinking.

"Look, I have to go in a minute, but tell me, why are you guys hiding in here?"

"I want to be with my daughter. If I do not go to America, I will never see her again. I could not bear that."

"So you're going to give up this life?"

"What life is it? A lie is what it is. I believe in democracy."

"We go on the boats tomorrow," Blaise added.

"Wow. God bless you on your journey and be sure to contact me." She rummaged through her bag until she found Steve's business card and phone number. "Here, this is all I have. Call this number and ask for Madelline Croft. It's my alias," she whispered. "I'll see you in America." She gave both men a kiss on the cheek and they regarded her affectionately as she shut the trap door. As she was crawling out, she heard Steve's voice inside the house. She quickly put on her wig and glasses and put the camera under her straw hat, lifting her head to see Steve's smiling face.

"You're amazing. How did you win him over?" Steve asked, pointing his thumb towards Theron.

"Um, well, charm," she said, still on her knees.

He knelt in front of her, whispering. "Well did you get it?"

She felt the hat on her head. There was no way she could show him the pictures of her. "No. The camera was not there."

"Not there? We came all the way here and..."

"I'm sorry. I know, it's disappointing." She looked down, frustrated, wishing she could share their accomplishment. "Look, let's go. We need to get back." She stood up, kissed Theron on his leathery cheek and thanked him.

When they had been peddling for a few minutes and were in a secluded area, Nina heard some rustling in the trees. She slowed down so Steve could catch up with her. "Do you hear something?"

They heard the rustling sound again.

"I think we're being followed," he said.

"What should we do?"

A man in a yellow uniform ran in front of Steve's trail, waving. Nina recognized that he was a soldier who carried a weapon. "Get on the back of my bike." Steve told Nina.

Nina dumped her bike on the ground, hopped on the back of Steve's and wrapped her arms around his waist.

"Hold on. Here we go."

As he whizzed forward, Nina looked behind them. The soldier had secured her bicycle and was darting after them.

"He has my bicycle. He's catching up to us," Nina said.

"Hold on. I'm gonna go faster."

Steve pedaled fast through difficult terrain, and when they hit a bumpy surface, they had to get off.

"Run, Madelline." He grabbed her hand, sprinting towards the direction of the resort. But the soldier raced in front of them with Nina's bicycle and jumped off, tumbling to the ground.

"Blaise," he yelled. "Blaise." He grabbed Steve's ankle causing him to trip.

Nina examined his face for the first time and realized that he was the soldier who had helped them to Amandine's cousin's house.

"Alain?" she said.

He nodded, then handed Nina a small, bound book with a red leather cover. "Amandine." He gave Nina back her bicycle as she stood there stunned and Steve gathered to his feet.

"Let's go home," he said.

If they had a comfortable camaraderie on the way to Haiti, the way home was juxtaposed by an awkward silence. Nina spent her time, thumbing through the red bound book that had many photographs of Amandine when she was a little girl and also had a personal diary that Nina did not dare read.

When they got off the plane in the States, Steve walked briskly through the airport towards the taxicab section. Nina followed him, hauling her suitcase, trying to keep up. Steve made a call and got in his limo with his chauffeur, Marcus.

Nina followed him in and shut the door. It was a dark night, but the streets of New York were bustling with energy.

"Look, I'm sorry this trip didn't work out. But this case is really important to me. It was worth a try. And who knows, maybe some of Amandine's other family members will come here and we will have many witnesses. Or maybe there's something in this diary that's consequential. What do you think?"

"I think it was strange that you knew the officer's name was Alain."

CHAPTER 7

Although Steve had thought they botched their investigation, Nina had the camera in her suitcase. She retrieved it from the pocket and immediately took the camera to a one-hour film, processing center, then waited for it to get developed in the dorm lobby and sat up on the desk with Anthony.

"So now tell me about this play you're in that you always have to be walking around in disguise?" he said. He had seen her in her Remmy disguise going in and out of the building for the past year. She had identified herself right away. Otherwise, she would not have been able to get in the building.

"It's an original. A girl pretends to be someone else to save her friend."

"And are you the star?"

"Hmmm. I guess you can say that."

Later when Anthony got busy checking in students, she slipped away and called her mother's place to speak to Amandine.

"I saw your father and brother."

"You did?" Her voice was excited. "Where are they?"

"Right now they are on a boat headed for America."

"What? This cannot be. My father is an important person in Haiti."

"Yes, but he has decided to leave it all to be with you."

"I do not understand."

"They were hiding in the compartment in the fisherman's house. They looked well and were eager to make the trip."

"Wait a minute. You went to Haiti? Back to the fisherman's house? What are you crazy? You could have been harmed."

"But we weren't. We thought we were being chased by a soldier on a bicycle, but it turned out it was Alain. He gave me your diary."

"He had my diary? That was in my bedroom. They must have ransacked our home." She was quiet for a moment. "Well, I guess it doesn't matter now. We won't go back there. I wonder if he read it."

"Why?"

"There's much about him."

"Oh."

"He was my first boyfriend." Her voice was sad.

"I'm sorry."

"No. Don't be. It is his choice to do the work he does. It could have been different for us. Anyway, I'm glad you have it." She paused. "So Nina, why did you go back to Haiti?"

"To get the camera."

"Why? Why are you doing all of this?"

"For you, my best friend. Remember the time I was really depressed during freshman year? I didn't feel like I fit in with all those college kids from wealthy families. Well, who made me feel important? Who made me feel that I was worth something? You did. You've always been there for me, Amandine. I've never had a friend like you."

"I never had a friend like you who would risk her life for me."

"Your problems are my problems. I couldn't imagine my life without my friend, Amandine, the one person besides my mother who really cares about my heart. Friendship like that is gold."

"Well no matter what happens, know that I owe my life to you."

"You don't owe me anything and I think we will win with this evidence."

"You do, really?"

"It is my deepest hope."

"What's up, girlfriend?" Remmy came on the phone next.

"All of my paychecks from McNamara are going to your bank account. How can I access them?"

"Hey, you make big bucks. I should take the money and try again in Vegas. I think I can win this time."

"I'm serious."

"You're always serious. Too serious, I think."

"Excuse me. But I'm trying to help Amandine, remember?"

"I know. And we all appreciate it. We do, Nina. You're all we talk about. How you're this remarkable heroine."

"I wouldn't go that far."

"I would," she said. "I'll have the money wired to you tomorrow. So how's my bro?"

"He's mad at me," Nina said quietly. "I mean at Madelline."

"Who's Madelline?"

"That's my newest identity."

"I don't even want to know about this one." She chewed gum while she was talking. "So why is he mad at you?"

"It's a long story. I think he's annoyed that I dragged him to Haiti."

"He went to Haiti with you?"

"Yes, with Madelline. For Amandine's case."

"You're starting to talk about yourself in the third person. This is scary." She cracked her gum. "But if my brother went with you to Haiti, you can bet he probably has a thing for you."

"Madelline isn't very attractive."

"Well, it sounds like he's seen beyond that."

"What happens when he finds out I'm really Nina?"

"He'll never forgive you. Steve never lies and he can't tolerate it."

Nina threw the wig on the floor and stomped on it.

An hour later, Nina picked up the photos at the processing center and took the envelope with the negatives to the park where she plunged onto a familiar bench that was unoccupied.

There she opened the envelope, grabbed the photos and searched through the various faces. She saw Amandine with her father in front of his mansion, arms around each other in fancy clothes. Next, was a picture of Arnaud shaking hands with an important government official as he was leaving a dinner at his home. Then she saw herself, carefree roaming about the beach with Amandine in their blue bikinis, and later, parading through the committee meeting. Nina took these pictures out of the bunch and put them in the side of her suit pocket.

The rest of the pictures greatly disturbed her. They were the ones Blaise took during the raid. The vivid depictions brought back the memories of that terrifying day in Haiti and further back to the time she and her mother fled as refugees when she was six, all in the name of freedom, all in the desire for a better life. Pained by the atrocities, she became sick in the smelly mouth of a nearby trash can, then wiped her lips with her sleeve. She grabbed one of the pictures and ripped it to shreds, then buried it inside an old pizza box.

"You know, I don't think it was a waste of time at all for us to go to Haiti. We were able to see the countryside and the people; even had our own brush with how it feels to be chased and running for our lives. I think this will help us to identify with Amandine and prepare an effective case," Nina said in the library, trying to get Steve's attention.

"We don't need to identify with her, Madelline, we are lawyers not actors. At least I'm not. But you, I'm not sure what you're all about with all your secrets." Steve had his back to Nina in the library the following morning as he was perusing some research for another case.

"What do you mean?"

"You express all these wonderful noble ideas about making a difference in the world and I love talking to you, but I get the feeling that you are hiding something from me. There's just been too much incongruity."

"What are you talking about?"

"Ms. Madelline Croft the Russian. Ms. Madelline Croft who hides her face behind thick, tinted glasses. Ms. Madelline Croft who knows her way around the streets of Port-Au-Prince, but she's never been there. Ms. Madelline Croft who knows a Haitian soldier named Alain."

She sat next to him, speaking softly. "I am Russian. And I do believe in my causes and in doing my work with love. I'm like you. I want to make the world a better place."

"And what would make the world better?"

"If all it had was love."

"And what about truth?"

"If all we had was love, then there would also be only truth. But unfortunately, not everyone acts out of love and so we all become vulnerable of being sucked into a murky web."

"Well don't get too sucked in, or you might not be able to get out."

"I realize that. And I know my behavior's been a bit peculiar at times, but I promise you that my intentions are out of love." She stood up, pacing the floor. "So are you still working on the case with me?"

"We couldn't get the evidence."

"So you just drop her? You've been to Haiti. You've seen first hand how people can be treated. How can you deny this? It doesn't matter if you don't like me, it is our responsibility as officers of law to see that justice is done."

"Don't put this on me. There are several other attorneys whom you can get to work with you." Then in a quieter voice, "And I didn't say I didn't like you, I just am not sure if I can trust you. I'm not sure what your motivations are." He walked closer to her. "So at what point Madelline, can we have a society of truth?"

"When we can have a society of love."

He nodded, deep in thought, but then turned to do his work. She felt the urge to go over to him and yank the soft brown curls on the back of his head. She wanted to bury her face into them and cry.

That night, she went home feeling lonely so she called Art in Connecticut and had an honest discussion with him about the predicament she was in.

"Do you think I'm terrible to tell all those lies?"

"No. No. You're doing this to save your friend. You're a beautiful person."

"But still, all this dishonesty it feeds on itself. It's so parasitic."

"But what can you do now? You've got to help her."

"Maybe Wess can do it himself."

"You said yourself, he is swamped. He simply doesn't have the resources or time to dedicate to this case. He's counting on you and it sounds like, so is Amandine."

She put her hands on her face. "I'm so confused. What should I do with these pictures?"

"You need to use them."

Nina walked to a copy center near NYU and rented a typewriter. She still had Natasia's old black typewriter at her dorm, but it was ancient and the type was unique. Nina needed to compose a letter that was not traceable. She handed her keys over to the desk clerk for collateral, then sat down at the keyboard in a black suit and composed the following letter:

Dear Steve Peterson, Esq.,

I would like to apologize for not showing up at your scheduled interview. Your intern, Madelline Croft, had left several messages for me, but I'm afraid to be a witness. I want to be an asset in helping in Amandine's case, but I would rather help behind the scenes. Over the past week, I was able to secure my camera, but at this point, I'd rather not disclose the manner in which I received it. Enclosed, are the photographs that we took the night Amandine fled to America. I'm certain these photographs will help your case.

Sincerely,
Nina Selinsky

When Nina finished with the letter, she signed it and typed Steve's name on a label that she pressed on the front of a large envelope. Then she stuffed the letter with the envelope from the photo center into a large manila envelope and sealed it closed. She arrived at the office around 3:00 p.m., lingered around the halls for awhile, then found the nerve to place the evidence on Steve's chair when the library was empty.

As Nina scurried back towards her own office, she passed another intern's cubicle. Her name was Louise Ritter. Steve was sitting on Louise's desk chatting with her and they were eating lunch out of Chinese food containers with chopsticks. When Nina walked by, they got silent. She turned in front of them and took a drink out of the fountain.

"How are you doing?" Steve said, suddenly standing beside her.

She looked at Louise and felt a lump, the size of an egg, growing in her throat. Louise was cute and bubbly, and Nina had her first taste of how it felt to be insecure of her appearance, her disguise having grown as part of her identity over the past several months. She had always taken for granted her beauty and realized now that she had used it for gain in almost every interaction. But now, she had to rely on her inner makings, and she prayed it was beautiful enough. But as she saw him flirting with Louise in a way he had not done with Madelline, she felt she was losing in this superficial world. A part of her wanted to go on being Madelline forever to prove that looks didn't matter. But the other part of her wanted to disrobe right there in the office, and let the beautiful lion free and untamed to ravage the great Steve Peterson.

"I've been thinking about what you said, and I'm with you on wanting to help Amandine."

"Really?"

"Yes. I want to help her in the name of love." He smiled, and Nina attempted a smile back, but then ran to her office, trembling about the most recent lie she had dumped on him, trying to picture his reaction upon reading her letter and looking at the photographs. So when she finally made it to her office, she closed her door and laid her head down on the desk. She had at least twenty notes on her desk from various people regarding other cases she was supposed to be working on. She just sat there, sick with frustration.

At around 5:30 p.m., she sauntered to the elevator, but remained stoical as she rode down to the lobby, staring at the numbers flashing brightly on every floor.

"Madelline I've been looking for you all day." She heard Steve say. He was sitting on the guard desk in the lobby the way she always did with Anthony. "But you weren't in the library'. Are you okay?"

She shrugged.

"I have something I need to share with you," Steve said, standing up. He was holding the envelope addressed to him by Nina Selinsky.

They went out to dinner at a trendy Latin American restaurant in the Village where they had Salsa music. When they finished dining, they reviewed the letter and the photographs that Steve had purportedly received from Nina Selinsky. She tried to act surprised as she recapped each photo.

"It is obvious to me from these photographs, that Amandine came from a prominent family in Haiti, and she risked her life to go to a committee meeting in support of a revolutionary cause which was raided by the Haitian military." Steve waved the pictures in front of his face like a fan. "These pictures are sad. I'm glad I'm working with you again." He examined a picture. "You know I didn't realize this before. But Amandine is gorgeous."

"Why are you always telling me this stuff?"

"Hey, I'm just a regular guy, a regular guy who likes to look at beautiful women. Why, do you think that's shallow?"

"It depends," she said.

"Good lawyer answer."

"Look, if you love someone, then you should love their soul, otherwise you're building a foundation of love on sand. But if the person you love happens to be beautiful, then you have been blessed with a special gift."

He stared at Madelline, caressing her cheek with his hand. There was soft, Latin music playing and Steve led Nina to the dance floor near the bar. They were the only occupants on the floor. They danced closely and Nina allowed herself to loosen up as she buried her head into his chest.

She could feel his breath on her neck and in her ears. Then he put his mouth on her mouth, kissing her lips softly while removing her glasses. She ran her hands through his curls as she kissed him back on his lips and breathed in the smell of his wonderful cologne.

But before they could open their eyes, she grabbed her glasses out of his hand and rested them back on her face.

He looked up. "Please. Madelline. Take off your glasses. I want to see your face."

She shook her head, backing away from him.

"Okay, it doesn't matter." He rubbed his hand through his hair. "It's just that. I don't know what it is."

A few moments later, he paid the bill, took Nina's hand and hailed the limo.

In the morning, she stopped by his penthouse to go over a strategy for the evidence. While she was in the living room, he carried in a tray with eggs, toast and some coffee. There was a vase with a bouquet of lilacs in the center. He placed the tray in front of her and sat next to her watching her eat.

"It's wonderful, thank you." She tried not to talk with her mouth full. "I especially like the cheese in the eggs."

"It's a combination of mozzarella and Jack." He gestured with his hands as he talked. "This is refreshing. Most women don't like to eat cheese and other great food. They're always watching their weight. But I think food can be passionate." He got closer to her, grabbing the sides of her face with his palms. "You are a beautiful person, cloistered in layers upon layers." He tugged on her barrette. "I'd really love to see your face and your hair."

She moved away, blushing. "Please. Let's get back to the case."

He picked up a piece of the toast and devoured it, using his hands and mouth, making her laugh uncontrollably.

He dusted off the crumbs on his pants. "Okay, what do you think we should do next?"

Nina reflected for a moment. "I don't know. I wish we could find some of the people in these photographs and get their testimony about what happened," she said.

"I'm not going back to Haiti."

"No. But how about Little Haiti? I'm sure some of these people are there. We can ask Amandine."

"That's a great idea." He looked up at Nina. "For the first time in this case, we have some real, physical evidence that we can work with thanks to Nina Selinsky. Do you think she went back to Haiti to get the camera or what?"

Nina shrugged.

"And I don't presume she's in the pictures because she's not Haitian. Unless, she took her pictures out."

"Why would she do that?"

"Well, she doesn't want to be involved in the hearing in any way. I might subpoena her."

"I can't believe what you're saying. If she doesn't want to, why make her miserable? We have faces of other witnesses. We can find them."

Later that afternoon, Nina received permission from McNamara to take a few days off so she could go to Florida. They intended on giving copies of the photographs to Wess Salinger to see if he had any information on any of these refugees. In the meantime, Nina and Steve waited in line at a travel agent to get their plane tickets to Miami.

A few days later, at the set of dusk, they were in a rent-a-car outside the Refugee Clinic in Little Haiti when they saw a young Haitian woman come down the street and stand in front of the double black doors. She looked like the woman with full hair and the silk scarf around her neck. She had lain on Amandine's lap while they were in the wooden boat on the coast of Port-Au-Prince. Nina studied her, remembering how Amandine had stroked that beautiful dark hair. The woman finished a soda pop, tossed it into a garbage can then walked into the clinic.

"That's Amandine's friend," Nina said with her hand on the door opener, ready to get out and talk to her.

Steve flipped through the pictures. "I think you're mistaken. I would have recognized her. She's not in any of these pictures."

"Still, I think I saw her with Amandine."

"When?"

"I don't know. Maybe during Christmas break."

"Why can't we just go in the clinic? I don't understand."

"I told you. Wess won't like it if I bring you in there. He doesn't know you."

"I'm working for the same cause."

"Still, you're a lawyer and, and he might feel threatened. You know he supervises all the law students. He might think you're trying to, I don't know, take over or something."

"You're not making any sense. There you go again, Madelline, always acting suspicious. I'm sure Wess Salinger would love to have another attorney helping him." He got out of the car.

Nina jumped out, following him to the doors. "Okay. Go speak to Wess if you have to. But please, please don't mention my name. Deal?"

He shrugged, flinging the door open. Nina waited outside, pacing up and down the sidewalk, hoping Steve did not ask Wess if a Madelline Croft had worked there.

After about twenty minutes, she saw Wess and Steve coming towards the front door. Nina quickly ran around the building, hiding as it started to get dark outside. She listened as they exchanged a few words.

"You don't know how happy we are to have you here," Wess told Steve. "Are you any relation to Remmy Peterson?"

Nina's knees were shaking.

"Yes. That's my sister. How do you know her?"

"She didn't tell you? She's been so helpful on the Amandine Dubois case."

"Remmy? Remmy Peterson?"

Just then. Amandine's friend came out of the clinic and walked around the building, past Nina, carrying a large red, tote bag. It was dark outside now, and she didn't notice Nina crouching against the white stucco. She walked at a fast pace and Nina followed about ten yards behind her.

She climbed up the fire escape on the side of an apartment building that led up to a sixth floor window which she entered.

Nina climbed up the fire escape with her black pumps dangling on the tips of her fingers.

When she reached the window, she pulled it up and found it unlocked. She opened it as she peered around, it was dark, but she knew she was in a kitchen. She turned around and jumped down, backwards, to the floor. The apartment was quiet and dark. She tiptoed around the wall, but saw no one in the living room. Then she hid against the wall right next to the back room. After a few seconds, she poked her head in the doorway. She could see a Haitian family in there, sitting on the bed. Then on the floor, were other refugees. Amandine's friend was pulling supplies out of the bag such as soap and combs which were complimentary from the Refugee Clinic and distributing them to the people who accepted them with open hands. They called her Cerise and revered her with adoration as they kissed her on both of her cheeks. As Nina watched from behind the doorway, she accidentally dropped her shoe on the ground making a small clamor. Cerise looked in her direction, grabbed the bag and darted for the door.

Nina slid across the floor in her stocking feet, then quietly slipped through the front door. Breathing heavily, she ran down the front staircase. She sat down on the lobby floor, trying to catch her breath. She looked out the front window and could see Steve circling around in the car, looking for her. She knew he would disapprove of her investigation and put a stop to it, so she ignored him as she crouched in the corner of the dark lobby.

A few moments later, Cerise came down the steps of the apartment building. She carried the bag and her face was gaunt and her eyes, exhausted. She looked like a woman who had weathered a great deal of adversity. She walked at a fast pace and Nina followed after her, past the clinic and onto a city bus.

CHAPTER 8

Cerise's apartment was in a neighborhood of Miami that was known for its gangs. There were kids in the streets, listening to loud music. She brushed past the kids like it was her routine, and they in turn, greeted her with the same nonchalance. She gave a homeless guy some change as he opened the door to her building. The man stuffed the money into his pocket; Cerise entered her building and Nina lost sight of her.

Nina picked up speed as she zipped past the kids, grabbing the door that was still ajar from the moment Cerise had entered. As she stepped into the apartment building, Nina nearly lost her breath for lack of oxygen. There was everything but steaming hot coals in the corner of the lobby that reminded Nina of the sauna bath she sometimes took with Natasia at her condo. Cerise clutched her tote bag as she got into the elevator. The doors started to close so Nina pushed on the side of the door and slid through. When Cerise pushed the tenth floor button, Nina could see her hands were trembling.

"Are you okay?" Nina whispered, hoping she spoke English.

"I am fine." The girl spoke in a deep voice that was unexpected. Nina followed her to the tenth floor, then stepped off the elevator after her. Nina stood in the hallway and watched as the girl entered her apartment. Her door had peeling wood chips that had crumbled to the floor. There was a top bolt and a bottom lock for which she rummaged through her tote bag to find the keys.

Nina continued to crouch around the corner until she finally saw the girl enter her apartment. She heard a series of locking noises, and then, it was silent.

Nina paced down the hallway three or four times before she took out a pack of gum, stuffing three pieces in her mouth, chewing vehemently. She hadn't smoked in months, and she was nervous. There were no windows in the hallway and Nina thought she would perish from poor ventilation. She took off her suit jacket and tied it around her waist, gasping for air to reach her lungs while she knocked on the girl's door. She heard faint footsteps moving closer, then she heard that deep voice again.

"Who is it? Who's out there?"

Nina paused for a moment to gather her thoughts, but she could think of nothing brilliant or encouraging to say. "Hi, I'm Nina, Amandine's friend. Hi. I'm Remmy, a rich girl with a cause. Hi. I'm Madelline, here to help refugees. Nina Selinsky?" There was no use for introductions, so she just said, "Listen, I'm here to talk to you about something. Can I just have a moment?"

"I do not open the door for anybody."

Nina thought back to Natasia and could hear her mother's voice; "The Russians are coming back to take us away!" Nina still had nightmares of Russian men, dragging her out of her little flat in Brooklyn. "Look, I understand. You don't have to open the door. I can talk to you through the door."

"Through the door?"

"Yes, if you don't mind."

"Who are you? The INS?"

Nina laughed. This was going to be a long night. "No. No. I'm a student. My name is Nina." She decided for the truth as she took out some more gum and blew a bubble. "I have some questions."

"I am not answering any questions."

"Why not?"

"I am not getting into any trouble."

"I understand. Listen, are you friends with Amandine Dubois?"

"I will not answer your questions."

Nina sat down against the door of the girl's apartment. She could feel some of the wooden splinters poking against her back. "Okay, you don't have to answer any questions. Just let me tell you a story. Can I tell you a story?"

There was no answer.

"Once upon a time, there was this young woman from Haiti, around twenty-two. She had dreams of being a physician in America and studied very hard. She went to NYU for three years and was an honor student. She was trying to get into medical school, but it turned out she couldn't finish her senior year of college. You see, she went back to Haiti to visit her father and while she was there, she decided to help her friends in their fight for democracy and attended a committee meeting with her brother Blaise and friend, Nina." Nina heard some shuffling behind the doorway. "That day, the military raided the meeting and arrested many of her friends. She fled for her life and hid in a secret compartment of a fisherman's cottage. When the coast was clear, the fisherman took her to a wooden boat that was headed for Florida. While she was in the boat, a young girl with a silk scarf around her neck was crying. She took the young girl in her lap, stroked her hair and comforted her." Nina talked slowly, enunciating her words. "Together, they made the journey to sea and with God's help, they made it safe to America." As Nina said this, she could hear soft crying in the background. "You see, Cerise, Amandine was caught by the INS and arrested. Now, she will be deported back to Haiti and will be in grave danger if she cannot prove her case for political asylum. All she needs are some friends to act as witnesses and help her with her case so that her life can be spared and so that she can return to school and someday be a wonderful, compassionate physician."

As Nina finished her story, she heard Cerise unlock the door. Nina was startled and stood up abruptly, turning around. Cerise was waving the silk scarf in front of her. "Amandine gave this to me." She coiled it around her neck, wiping her tears.

Nina put her arms around her, hugging her closely. "It's going to be okay," Nina told her in a whisper. "We're going to help Amandine and you and all of your friends, too."

At around 6:00 a.m. the next morning, Nina arrived at Steve's hotel in Delray Beach. There was a police car in front, making Nina nervous.

"What's going on?" Nina asked the doorman. He looked dapper in his uniform after Nina had spent most of the night in a coffee shop with Cerise in the gang district doing an asylum interview on Nina's cassette recorder. The doorman scrutinized Nina. Her clothes were rumpled.

"I'm not exactly sure what's going on. I think somebody's missing. Hey, you're Mr. Peterson's friend, aren't you?"

Nina nodded.

"Look, you better go see him. They're all up in his hotel room."

Nina looked up, averting her eyes to his gold buttons. "Who is up in his room?"

"The police, that's who."

Erica Axelrod

"The police!" Nina rushed to the elevator and pressed the button to the second floor, then vigorously pounded on the door. Steve flung it open.

"Madelline!" He grabbed her close to himself, putting his strong hands on her face. "Where on earth did you disappear to?"

Two cops were closing in on them.

"I didn't disappear. Well, I guess I did from you. I'm so sorry. I didn't even think of the fact that you might miss me. I guess I've been kind of a free bird and I didn't think..."

Steve put his arms around Nina, holding her tight. "You don't need to explain. I'm just glad you're okay," he whispered. He led Nina to the couch and helped her to sit down. "Do you need water or something?"

"No, I'm fine. Nothing happened to me."

"Well, then where've you been?" the cop asked in a not so soothing voice.

"I just went to work on our case. I was working in a coffee shop all night."

"Where?" The policeman had a pencil out and was reporting something in a small notebook.

"Rinkys Donuts. You can go ask the waitress, Dinah, she's been pouring us coffee all night."

"Who's we?" the officer said.

"A witness in our case. It's confidential," Nina said.

The officers packed up their stuff and headed for the door. They said something to Steve on their way out about how Nina should not be going to places like Rinkys in the middle of the night. Then they left.

144

She glanced over at Steve. "I followed that young woman we saw with the soda pop in front of the Refugee Clinic. I followed her to this apartment after you left and I climbed through the window."

"What?" He gasped. "You can't do that."

"Well, I did. Because I knew something clandestine was going on there."

"And was it?"

Nina nodded.

"What?" He moved closer.

"Somebody is harboring about fifteen refugees there."

Steve's mouth fell open. "Any that you recognized?"

"Yes," Nina said. "And the woman told me that these refugees all know Amandine."

"What do you mean she told you?" Steve said. "You spoke to her?"

"I followed her to her home when she came out of the apartment building. She told me Amandine saved her life."

Steve came over to Nina, sat down next to her and pulled out his pen and legal pad. "Tell me exactly what she said."

"She said she didn't know how to swim, and when they came close to American soil, they could not get close enough to the shore and they had to swim there. Well, Amandine and the boatman gathered a log from the boat, put Cerise on top of it and Amandine hauled her in. She wants to testify for Amandine, but she is an undocumented immigrant and if she goes into court, she'll be arrested. They all will. It won't work."

Steve slammed his fist on the table. "There must be something we can do."

"I want to help all of them. You should have seen them, living all together in such crowded conditions, hiding for their lives."

"Did you tell her maybe we can process her claim too?" Steve asked.

"Yes, but she said that would be voluntarily giving herself over to the authorities. Currently she is innocuous. She is working under the table at Rinkys," she whispered. "Technically, she can go on living like this forever as long as she doesn't get caught."

"But it's no life, living dishonestly, afraid all the time."

"The alternative is severe persecution in Haiti." Nina reminded him.

She went to the window, staring out at the sea, looking at the powerful motion of the ebb and flow, yielding hopeful souls to freedom.

When Wess Salinger confirmed that he recognized many of the refugees in the photographs, he told Steve it would be excellent evidence for Amandine's case. However, he explained that the others would have to make the choice of either voluntarily submitting themselves to the authorities and going for political asylum, which could risk deportation or they could choose to go on living as undocumented immigrants. The choice was theirs. But he agreed that if any decided to go for asylum, they could corroborate each other's story and would serve as excellent witnesses for each of the cases. He told Steve that he would like to get in touch with Remmy right away about the photographs because she was leading the case. Steve had kept his promise and had not mentioned the name of Madelline Croft.

"So what's the deal with my sister working on this case? Did you know about this?" Steve asked Nina, later that day.

Nina had spent the day researching in the library as many articles as she could find on political persecutions in Haiti. She made copies of these articles to use as evidence in Amandine's case. She was sitting on Steve's couch, pretending to read the clippings, but meanwhile, trying to figure out a plan to gloss over the newest hole in her lie, reminding her a little of Swiss cheese when you stick your fingers in the holes and pull it apart.

"Um, yes, I thought you knew that Remmy was working on the case. I thought that's why you were interested, too."

"This is getting ridiculous." He paced back and forth. "Remmy would never be interested in this case. The girl doesn't even know what asylum means." He had his hands in his pocket.

"Look, she's been working on it since the beginning. That's why you haven't seen her in the office. She's been here in Florida, working on the case."

"I don't believe it."

"Would you like to go to lunch?"

Remmy met them at Beachers, the popular restaurant by the shore where Natasia had won the limbo contest on New Year's Eve.

Remmy came over to their table, giving her brother a big smooch on the cheek.

"I thought that's how you would greet him?" Nina said, chuckling. "A good actress always studies her subject," she said to Remmy, when Steve went to the bathroom.

"You're definitely a much, much," she enunciated, "less attractive version of me. My brother is so funny. He can date any girl he wants." She examined Nina through her ice tea glass.

"Look, I didn't come here to be insulted."

"But I'm not insulting you."

"But in a way you are," Nina said. "I can't explain it. It's like this costume is a part of me now."

"Okay, I can see that. Like the Stanislavski method or something."

Nina laughed. "Look, I've arranged this lunch because Wess Salinger told Steve that Remmy Peterson was the lead legal expert on Amandine's case."

"Wait a minute. Steve met Wess? But didn't Wess see you? Didn't he call you Remmy?"

"No. Please, I'm not that dumb. I didn't go in the clinic with Steve. I've been doing other research and questioning witnesses."

148

"Cool. I've been working at the bagel shop. I made, get this, fifty-eight bucks in tips yesterday."

"Congratulations."

Steve came back to the table.

Over the next few days, Steve and Nina worked diligently throughout each night, explicating asylum theories. Steve ordered room service while Nina reviewed the tape recording of Cerise. The asylum hearing was scheduled for Monday, August 10, 1993.

Meanwhile, Amandine came over to their room for Steve to meet with her and do an extensive asylum interview, and to cover any holes in the first interview. Nina sat by his side, impressed with his thoroughness. She could tell he had spent much time with Wess, going over the methodology of asylum interviews. Amandine was eager to finish because afterwards, they had planned on going to Cerise's apartment for a reunion.

But when they arrived at Cerise's apartment and knocked at the door, there was not an answer.

"The INS take her," the homeless man told them, in front of the lobby.

A week later, Wess Salinger was working on Cerise's asylum case. She was released from custody and allowed to move back to her apartment and received a work card to continue employment at Rinkys. Nina had already conducted a taped interview with Cerise and with her permission, gave the cassette to Wess so that he could use it to prepare for the case.

While Cerise was out of custody and back in her apartment, she was no longer allowed to visit with the refugees to give them supplies. Any problems with the INS could hinder her asylum claim, so it was Remmy Peterson, the real Remmy Peterson, who began to assume that role. So as not to confuse anyone, she told Wess Salinger that her name was Madelline Croft.

Now that Steve and Nina were back in New York, Nina was swamped at work, catching up on other immigration cases, and only had time to work on Amandine's and Cerise's cases in the evenings.

She spent almost every evening in the living room of Steve's penthouse their first week back, preparing for the cases.

She even filled a small bag with clothes, accessories and toiletries, and toted a carton of files containing all of her legal notes to bring to the penthouse.

"Where you off to?" Anthony had asked her as Steve greeted her at the door, and carried her belongings.

"Rehearsal," she mouthed in his direction, then louder, "if anyone asks about me, here is a number where they can reach me." She handed him a piece of paper with Steve's number.

"I hear you girl." Anthony turned towards Steve. "Hey, you take care of this one. She's going to be a judge someday."

Steve paused. "A judge you say?" Steve winked at Nina affectionately as he carted her bag and carton of files into his limo.

"Looks like you're movin' up in the world!" Anthony yelled and whistled. The limo drove down MacDougal Street, past Washington Square Park. As

Nina rode in the black, swanky vehicle, she peeked out of the window and saw the chess players. Charlie was still hunched in the corner, playing against an elderly man. There was not much of a crowd today.

Later that afternoon, Steve and Nina went out to lunch with Soloman Horowitz. Nina had called him beforehand to tell him that Steve thought her name was Madelline Croft, and that it was a long story, but it was all for justice. Soloman liked the sound of the endeavor and agreed to meet them at a deli in Park Slope. He was not getting around much these days and wanted to be near his home.

In the beginning of the lunch, they discussed their cases, and told Soloman how they had photographs and how Amandine and Cerise corroborated each other's story as witnesses.

"I see." He nibbled on a corned beef on rye. "They make the best sandwiches in the city. Cream soda, please." He told the waitress.

Nina nibbled on a sour pickle. "So Mr. Horowitz, what do you think?"

"What do I think? I think the two of you are doing a wonderful job." He looked at his glass. "I need some ice. They never give enough ice." He jiggled his glass, studying the contents. "Look, I think you have enough evidence to get asylum for these gals, but...more ice please," he told the waitress.

Steve and Nina were leaning forward eager to be revealed the wisdom of the great Soloman. "But?" Nina asked.

"But, I am not the judge. I should be the judge, but I'm not."

"So what are you saying Mr. Horowitz? You think we need more?" Steve asked, picking apart his pastrami and making little sandwiches out of the mounds of meat.

"This guy doesn't know how to eat a deli sandwich," he told Nina pointing his thumb at Steve. "Anyway, the answer to your question is that you could always have more."

"More of what?" Nina asked.

"More of anything." He lifted his glass to receive a hill of ice. "You see. You never stop. You strive for perfection as if," he took a bite and chewed a bit, "as if it were your own life."

Soloman Horowitz spent the rest of the lunch telling stories about some of the remarkable cases he had won in his long, distinguished career. He had even brought an old scrapbook with him and pulled it out so he could show his past accomplishments.

"That one here was a refugee from China."

Steve flipped through the book, admiring the articles and photographs of the hundreds of people Soloman Horowitz helped. "Do you remember all of these people?"

"Each and everyone of them. They become part of your soul."

Steve smiled, turning to the last page, mesmerized. "Who is this beautiful woman?"

Nina grabbed the book out of his hand. There was a picture of Natasia and a little girl, in black and white, standing in front of Soloman's brownstone.

"That was my favorite client of all." He winked at Nina and retrieved his book.

Later as they were walking away from the deli towards the limo, Steve said, "What an incredible man."

"Oh, he is like a second father to me."

"I think he is right. I think we need to keep gathering more evidence." He opened the door to his limo and helped her inside. "I think we need an independent witness. Someone who does not have any personal interest in the case, someone who is not a refugee." The driver turned on the ignition. "The penthouse, Marcus."

Steve joked around with Marcus the whole way back to his home about sports and getting season tickets to the Yankees that they were going to attend together. Nina listened intensely, getting yet another perspective of Steve's character as she watched him treat his employee as a pal. It is not that she had thought he would be particularly pompous, as he was immersed in philanthropic causes and ideals. But she had found that sometimes people could get so caught up in their causes, that they lose sight of the people nearest to them. She was pleased to see that Steve remained true.

At the penthouse, Steve pulled out a mobile blackboard and set it in the middle of his living room then used colored chalk to jot down the elements of political asylum.

ASYLUM: Person must prove that he or she had a well-founded fear of persecution based on political reasons in their country in order to be granted political asylum.

"Okay, we know from the cases we have researched that a refugee must have a 'well-founded' fear of persecution. Therefore, it helps to have one's personal fear substantiated by objective standards such as what the political climate is in that country, and whether the refugee was a known dissenter of the country's politics," Nina said pointing to the element of 'well-founded' with a long stick. Nina took a moment, skimmed through her files, then retrieved some of her typed notes. "According to Amandine's testimony, the authorities became aware of her involvement to support democracy."

"But how can we prove that the authorities knew Amandine is a deserter?"

"In Amandine's testimony, she said her brother told her that the authorities knew about her and would be coming after her and then they chased her at her cousin's house with machetes."

"Yes. I understand that. But it would be good to have corroborating testimony from an independent witness."

"We have photographs of Amandine at the meeting."

"Yes, but that doesn't prove that the authorities saw her there."

Nina threw down her stick. "Whose side are you on?"

"Yours, I mean, Amandine's. I'm just trying to point out any holes."

Nina sat down and tried to think of something brilliant to say. Her mind was chasing itself in circles. "Maybe we could call Amandine to see if anyone else heard her brother say that the authorities knew about Amandine's desertion."

"Possibly, possibly." He walked back and forth. "Someone did report being with Amandine that night; the mysterious Nina Selinsky, remember?"

Nina nodded.

"She's afraid to testify, yet somehow she was daring enough to get the photos out of Haiti." He bit his lip. "It just doesn't make any sense. I will find her and I will subpoena her, with or without your cooperation."

"How are you going to find her?"

Steve stood up. "I'm going to McNamara's to question Yvonne Lindell-Frank about Ms. Selinsky. Maybe she still has her file with her name and address."

"I don't think that's necessary. We have so much evidence, we don't need..."

"What do you mean it isn't necessary? Your hero, Soloman, said we can't have too much evidence."

"We don't need her; we have Cerise."

"We need everything." Steve left the penthouse as Nina stood there feeling badly that Steve would waste his time. She knew Frank would not have a Nina Selinsky file.

An hour later, the phone rang.

"Hello," Nina said.

"Hi, I'm a reporter, Lloyd Carter, from the NYC Gazette. We've just got word that the millionaire,

Arnaud Dubois and his son have entered the United States and we'd like an official statement. Can I speak to his lawyer, Steve Peterson?"

Nina felt flutters in her stomach as she reached for a chair. "Well, um, Steve, he's not here at the moment. Can I have him call you?"

"Sure, uh, who am I speaking to?"

"Oh, this is, um, Madelline Croft."

"Madelline Croft? Are you working on the case with Mr. Peterson?"

"Well, yes,"

"Oh great. Well, then why don't you go ahead and give me a statement. We want to get this story out as soon as possible."

"Can I ask what the hurry is about?"

"What the hurry is? Are you kidding? The wealthiest man in Haiti on a refugee boat. This is big news."

"But where is he?"

"He was picked up by the coast guard at sea with his son and some other refugees."

Nina slumped in her chair. "You mean Arnaud Dubois and his son are at the Detention Center?"

"Yeah. And he had Steve Peterson's business card in his possession. Is Mr. Peterson, in fact, his lawyer?"

"Um, yes." Nina answered quietly, rubbing her temples.

"So then it would be safe to say that Mr. Peterson will be filing a political asylum claim on Arnaud's behalf."

"I don't know," Nina responded. "I need to speak to him."

"Well please call me when you have more information."

After Nina hung up the phone with Lloyd Carter, reporters began calling the penthouse continuously. Nina maintained composure as she tried to steer them away until Steve returned. When Steve came back, she updated him on the information and referred all calls to him because he was the lead attorney. Nina felt giddy as she watched Steve pace the floor, manipulating tough questions and evading other ones. In the evening, reporters came by to take Steve's picture. Nina felt like she was being swirled into the eye of a tornado, but she felt vivacious. And that night, as she was standing on the balcony, Steve came over and kissed the back of her head, wrapping his arms around her as they watched the sun set over the city.

"You see that city down there?" he said. "That city is ours. Isn't it beautiful?" He turned her around and quickly yanked off her glasses, then removed the wig from her head and stood there gaping as her long blonde hair draped around the contours of her beautiful face.

"You are Nina Pavlova." His mouth remained open as he ran his fingers through her luxurious hair. "It was you all along?" He had tears in his eyes. "The soul and the mind and now this precious gift." He scooped her into his arms, and carried her into his bed on top of his cool, green sheets. She let him unbutton each gold button on her suit, as he kissed her breasts and her neck. He pulled the padding from her suit and tossed it to the side of the bed, wrapping his arms around her tiny waist. Then he moved on top of her, caressing her and making love.

In the morning, she lay curled in his arms, staring at his sleeping eyes. She touched his long lashes with her finger and outlined his rugged, handsome bone structure until she came to his square jaw, so prominent in the day time and now preciously humble, resting on his pillow.

He opened his eyes, pulling her towards him, kissing her head. "Wow, it's really true. I wasn't dreaming." She lay on him quietly, kissing his bare chest.

"So what is it all about Nina? Why the charade?" He spoke softly.

"I wanted to help my friend."

He sat up abruptly with erect posture. "Amandine is your friend?"

She nodded.

"Then you're the Nina we've been looking for. You're the missing witness." He jumped out of bed, pacing.

Nina thought he looked incredibly sexy, and wished she could forget about it all momentarily and make love again, but she knew that she could not. She sat up with the soft, down comforter wrapped around her naked body. "Let's just forget about this."

"No. It's okay. It all makes sense now. That's why you knew your way around Haiti. You were there. You did get the camera, but why did you lie to me?" He looked at her, hurt.

She did not answer.

"Look, it's okay. It's all out in the open now. You'll testify and no one will even know that you were the girl helping on the case."

Nina stood up still wrapped in the makeshift toga. "No, you could get into trouble. A lawyer who knowingly tampers with evidence like that can get disbarred."

He looked down, sorrowful.

"But don't worry about it, because I'm not the missing witness. It was another girl who went to Haiti."

He moved to her on his knees holding her hands, kissing them. "This does not matter to me as much as you. I love you. I want an honest relationship."

Tears swelled up in her eyes. "You would risk your law license and everything you worked for to protect me?"

He looked at her eyes, adoringly. "Yes."

She pulled away from him. "Well, you don't have to, because I'm not the Nina who went to Haiti. That was Nina Selinsky." She went into his bathroom and slammed the door, then sat on his toilet seat and cried.

But he did not jimmy the door open this time because the phone rang. Nina could hear his conversation through the door.

"Hello...Dad, hi. Good morning...No I haven't seen the paper yet...Really? Wow! Well, I better step outside and get it."

While he was on the phone, Nina composed herself, then threw on his jersey and a pair of shorts so she could make a run to the newsstand. She purchased the NYC Gazette, then staggered toward the penthouse with her head plunged into the headlines. On Friday, July 31, 1993, Steve Peterson was on the front page.

Still in his bedroom, Steve was naked and pacing as he ranted into the telephone. She shoved the newspaper in front of his nose. The headlines read, "Richy Rich helps Haitian Refugees!" Then it explained the legal theories of political asylum quoted by Steve Peterson, Attorney at Law.

"This article is more about you being the most eligible bachelor in New York than it is about the plight of Arnaud."

"That's the media for you. They'll spin it anyway that sells. Look, that was McNamara on the phone, he wants to talk to me and my sister for some reason." He leaned closer. "Who does McNamara think you are?"

She bit her nails. "Um, your sister."

They got dressed in a hurry, then rode the limo to McNamara's office. When they stepped out onto the curb, reporters swarmed around them. Steve told them he would not be answering any more questions at this time. And they walked at a fast pace up to the office, slamming the door shut as they passed the receptionist's desk.

The office was alive, attorneys engaged in frenetic activity. Everyone was scurrying around the office and phones were ringing maniacally. As Nina and Steve walked down the halls, people badgered them with questions.

"You two better get into McNamara's office right now. He's got Martin McNamara in there with him and they have a lot of questions." Lindell-Frank warned them as she pointed her finger under Nina's nose.

They stepped into Jim McNamara's office. He was sitting in front of his desk like a client and Martin McNamara, the owner of the firm, was positioned behind Jim's desk. They rose to their feet as Nina and Steve walked in and introductions were made accordingly.

"Ms. Peterson, I hear you have been working on cases that are outside our office on our watch and our paycheck," Martin said. "Is that right?"

"No. I put in all of the hours I am required to. The other work, I do on my own time." Nina touched the barrette in back of her hair, making sure it was holding up the red wig.

"Well, Mr. Salinger called to thank me for, how did he put it, 'lending' you to their organization this summer. So I see you were down there, processing claims when you were supposed to be here," Jim said.

"I asked you if I could go to Florida."

"You said it was vacation."

"Well, for me it was. I enjoy helping refugees."

"It doesn't fit our profile," Jim said.

"And now, reporters are asking us all kinds of questions because they know the two of you are working on some big wig from Haiti's case and they think you are doing it out of our office," Martin said. "We need to set them straight."

Steve rubbed his chin. "Do you know what Arnaud Dubois did for a living in Haiti?"

They shook their heads.

"He sold almost all the produce from Haiti to the States like plantains and bananas. He was the wealthiest man in the country."

"So why'd the guy get on a boat to come here?" Martin asked, truly interested.

"Principles," Nina said, raising her eyebrows.

"Are we supposed to care about this?" Jim asked, looking at the two of them, back and forth.

"You could get a lot of good publicity if you backed us on this case," Steve said.

"You're kidding." Jim snorted through his nose.

But Martin leaned forward. "How so?"

"Read the papers." Steve pushed a paper across the desk. "The people of New York are very sympathetic to Arnaud. They want to see him get asylum. Your firm could get a lot of notoriety if it supported this," Steve said.

"On the other hand, if you fire me or refuse to let Steve use your facilities, the media would probably get word of this, and you may be looked upon in a bad light," Nina added.

"This is unbelievable," Jim said.

"No wait a minute. They may have a point," Martin said. He had a nasal voice, a balding head and white patches of hair behind each of his ears in even distribution.

162

Nina stared at the patches. She thought that if she slightly tugged on them, they might come off. "Well, what can we do to help you?" Martin asked.

They went to Steve's penthouse to review the legal theories, the physical evidence that was secured and the potential witnesses they had interviewed.

Finally, Martin and Jim stood to leave. And as Jim straightened his father's tie in the foyer, Nina could hear Martin whispering, "You know, Jim, this is good. This is really good."

That evening, Nina and Steve lay in bed watching the six o'clock news, showing Martin McNamara handling questions at a press conference about Arnaud Dubois.

"Unbelievable. You would never know that he just learned about this case only three hours ago," Steve said.

"Do you think we did the right thing?" Nina said.

Steve put his arm around her. "Definitely. McNamara has incredible resources and manpower."

"But we'll lose control. And they might not do a good job."

"No. I'm co-counseling with Jim, and as far as he's concerned, he'd love to delegate the work on these cases."

As they finished watching the press conference, the phone rang. It had been much more subdued today so Nina welcomed the intrusion.

"Hello." Nina said.

"Nina! This is your mother. Where are you right now? Whose phone number is this?"

"Mother, hi! Did you see the news? Did you see it was about Amandine's family?"

"Yes, I saw. We went to visit them at the Detention Center, a touching reunion. Made me think about your father," she said, somberly. "They told me what you did for them."

"They did?"

"Yes. I am very proud to have a daughter like you."

Nina smiled to herself. There was something about a mother's approval that seemed to validate your life. "Thank you."

"So where are you? Anthony at your dorm gave me this number."

"A friend's place," Nina said, admiring Steve from across the room, still uncertain if the evening together had been real.

Every time she had thought about his gentle touch on her body, she would shiver as if it were happening again and again. It saddened her that this fantasy had to be mired in the present reality of things.

"What kind of friend?"

"Hmmm? Oh, the attorney on Amandine's case."

"The hot one in the papers? Remmy's brother?"

"Yes, but he's not like Remmy, he's..."

"Sweetheart, be careful. Guys like that usually marry society girls."

"He's different. He said he loves me."

"Well. I just do not want you to get your beautiful heart crushed because I love you."

"I know what I'm doing. Trust me."

CHAPTER 9

On Saturday, Steve woke up early to make breakfast. Nina could hear him shuffling around the kitchen, chopping fruit, banging china, brewing coffee.

She got out of bed and draped herself with Steve's robe. It felt warm against her skin and she stuffed her hands in the pockets. She watched Steve's endeavors in the kitchen and smiled.

"You're so sweet to make breakfast for me," Nina said as she took some more china out of the cupboards to set the table. As they ate, they studied the morning newspapers. There had been more articles on the Arnaud Dubois case, mostly covering the press conference handled by Martin McNamara.

"Hey, did you see this?" Steve said handing over the front page to Nina.

Steve pointed to an article quoting Martin McNamara. It said, "McNamara & Associates has reason to believe that there are many refugees fleeing for their lives and seeking political asylum in this country. We encourage anyone who has had contact with the Dubois family in the past year to please get in touch with our office and perhaps they can receive free representation."

"What do you think? It's incredible, isn't it?" Steve said.

"Yes but, but I wonder what his motivation is." She rubbed her temples.

"Hey, who cares? Look what we started here. Because of our efforts, many refugees will be granted asylum in this country. I feel great! We're making a difference."

"It's beautiful."

Steve came around to where she sat and massaged her shoulders. "Hey, since there are so many other people involved in these cases now, I think we can afford a little break. What do you say about you and me going on a date this afternoon, a real date with no talk about the cases?" He nuzzled his face into her hair. Nina could feel the warmth of his breath on the back of her neck. She swiveled her body around to kiss him.

They arrived at the Peterson mansion in time for lunch on the patio. Harold and his wife, Midge, Steve's mother, Laney, Steve and Nina took their places around a circular glass table while an English maid served tea with little cakes and biscuits.

"Nina, it is so lovely to see you again," Laney said.

"Thank you."

"Are you getting excited to start law school?" Harold asked.

Nina gulped her glass of ice tea. "I begin my freshman year this fall."

"Oh, it is a time, freshman year, but I tell you, don't let yourself get too intimidated by the professors. They're just idealists, most of them."

"What's wrong with being an idealist?" Steve said.

"Oh, not this again. We know all about your newest endeavors. It was in all the papers that I don't read." Harold buttered his scone, one pat at a time, taking small bites, then wiping his mouth.

Steve became busy eating a bowl of gazpacho. "My grandfather only reads business and legal journals."

"Well, don't think for one minute that he didn't read all the papers the day his only grandson was in them," Midge said.

"I had to make sure that Steve was not too far out in left field that he couldn't be redeemed one day," Harold stated. Then he turned to Nina, "You see, some day Steve is going to be the head of Peterson & Peterson. Sure, he's having some fun right now, sowing his wild oats, experimenting, having some adventure. But we understand this lifestyle he's living right now is all very temporary."

Steve chuckled, but Nina could hardly speak during the rest of the meal. When she was finished, she excused herself and took a walk along the gardens alone in a lost expression, until Steve found her.

He wiped her eyes. "What's the matter?"

"It's, it's your grandfather," Nina said.

"My grandfather?"

"He doesn't want me here. He is only allowing me here because it's a 'temporary' situation, all part of your 'sowing your wild oats,'" Nina cried.

Steve placed his hands on her shoulders. "No, you're mistaken. My grandfather was talking about my career. He is really fond of you. And besides, it only matters what I think."

"And what do you think?" She sniffled.

"I think you give me a reason to get up everyday."

Nina smiled through her tears.

He reached for her hands. "Come on, let's go! I'm going to take you out on my boat. It will be wonderful out there. Just me and you, all alone."

They sat in plush chairs at the bow of the Peterson yacht that Steve had anchored in a quaint, little wharf. He told Nina that he always went there alone to think about his life.

The sun was hot beating down on Nina's white skin. Steve walked into the cabin and returned with sunscreen. He spread the white, coconut smelling lotion on Nina's face, then kissed her lips.

"I love how your fair coloring contrasts with your full, red lips."

"You make me sound like a porcelain doll."

He stared at her face, pensive. "No, you're more like one of those little, Russian dolls. When you first look at one, it's beautiful and you think that is all there is. Then you twist it open and there is another doll inside. And again, you twist that open and inside, yet another doll. There are layers upon layers of unknown territory underneath the smile of a Russian doll."

The city pulsated from the energy of the weekend visitors along Fifth Avenue. A lot of the wealthy city dwellers had escaped the weekend madness to go to their time-shares in the Hamptons or Fire Island. But Steve wanted to continue working on their cases so they were back in the city by 10:00 p.m., riding in the limo.

Steve was anxious to stop at a photo center to pick up some pictures he said that were being developed. When they pulled up to the store, Steve insisted that Nina wait in the limo while he went in to retrieve them. However, as soon as Steve entered the store, Nina followed him in.

She caught Steve's eye and he came right over to her followed by the owner, a skinny man with a curled up mustache.

"What are you doing? I thought you were waiting in the car," Steve said. He lightly grabbed Nina's hand. "Come on, let's go back." He looked at the owner. "Thank you for your work."

"What work? Why are you being so secretive now?" Then she turned to the owner. "What kind of pictures did you develop?" Her hands were on her hips.

"Excuse me, ma'am. I don't think I should get involved in this." He handed a package to Steve and walked behind his desk, staring at Nina. "Hey, do I know you from somewhere? Where have I seen you?"

"I don't know. I'm sorry. I don't recall ever meeting you," she said quietly.

"Hmmm. No. I'm sure I've seen you somewhere. I would never forget that face."

Steve winked at her salaciously, put his arm around her and led her to the limo with the package in the crux of his other arm. Nina was quiet on the way back to the penthouse as Steve chatted with Marcus.

When the limo pulled up to the penthouse at around 11:00 p.m., they were greeted by a crew of reporters.

"What's going on?" Nina asked. "Don't these people sleep?"

"I don't know. Just walk straight past them and don't answer any questions." Steve grabbed the package and the two of them walked briskly to the door.

Nina looked straight ahead, averting her eyes from the reporters. However, she managed to overhear some of their questions as she scurried past the doorman.

"Who is the woman with you Mr. Peterson?" one had asked. "Are you still the most eligible bachelor in New York or are the two of you seeing each other romantically?" "Do you have any idea what the count is now of the number of refugees who are being represented by McNamara & Associates?"

Nina stiffened and looked at Steve. "Did you hear that? They wanted to know the count of refugees who are being represented." She put her hands to her mouth. "Is it possible that we have turned McNamara & Associates into a philanthropic law firm?"

When they arrived at the penthouse, Randy and Nicholas were sitting on the floor in the hallway. Randy was not in uniform and Nicholas was dressed in a sport coat and some tan chinos.

Nina went running over to Nicholas. "It's so good to see you." She hugged him and introduced him to Steve. "This is my very dear friend, Nicholas. We go back a long time."

Steve shook hands, then turned to Randy. "Hey, I know you. You're the one who was looking for a Nina the night you came to the library over at McNamara's."

Randy stuck out his hand. "Yes, Randy Dombrowsky. Nice to see you again." They shook hands.

"So is this the Nina you were looking for?" He put his arm around Nina's waist.

Randy scrunched up his nose, looking very confused.

"No. I think it was the other Nina. You know, Nina Selinsky. The one who went to Haiti with Amandine." Nina stepped in front of Randy, her face almost kissing him.

Randy shrugged. "Yeah right. Nina Selinsky."

Steve eyed them, incredulously. "So where is she, Ms. Selinsky?"

"I don't know. She's a bit wacky. Could be anywhere." He smiled.

Steve went into his penthouse, turning on the news as the others remained in the hall.

"Why'd you come here?" Nina asked.

"We were looking for you. Your mother told us where you were. We missed you, Ms. Selinsky." He did a belly laugh, poking Nicholas in the side.

"Come on Nina. Get a drink with us." Nicholas wrapped his arm around her waist.

Steve was looking at them from his sofa inside the penthouse. Nina pulled away from Nicholas, and whispered, "Let me talk to him. He seems very annoyed. He's usually not like this." She moved slowly into the penthouse, leaving the others in the hallway. There was a reporter on the television with a bouffant. She was interviewing a legal scholar. "Isn't it true, Professor Pinkney, that most political asylum claims are handled by the Refugee Clinic in Miami?"

"Yes."

"So then why this sudden interest by McNamara?"

"Well as you know, Steve Peterson and his sister Remmy, recruited the owners of the firm to take an interest in the plight of Haitians. You see the clinic in Miami does an excellent job, but they don't have the resources to help everyone." He talked slowly. "But with McNamara's resources, why many refugees can be helped."

"Is this the way of the future?"

"We can hope. Never before have we seen such dedication from the wealthy and powerful helping the desperate and indigent in the practice of law, and we have Steve and Remmy Peterson to thank."

Nicholas and Randy were watching the news from the hallway.

Steve waited for them to come in.

"This is incredible," Randy said. "You should've seen all those fancy attorneys today, scrambling around for INS forms."

Steve laughed, but Nina could feel that he was distant.

"Look Steve, these guys are going to get a beer. Do you want to go?" Nina asked.

He rubbed his temples. "No. I'm sorry. I can't. I've got to get some sleep. I've got way too much work to do tomorrow." He looked over at Nina. "You go ahead. Go and have some fun for the both of us."

Nina tucked Steve into bed, shut out his light and promised she would be back in an hour. Then she headed to one of her old, stomping grounds at NYU, the bar called "Sticky Suds."

They slipped into a wooden booth and ordered a pitcher of beer. Randy, an expert at not allowing the head to overflow, filled up each of their mugs as Nina decided to reveal to them her entire story. It felt cathartic to tell the truth.

Nicholas' eyes were wide. "I can't believe all of the things that have happened to you. You're in deep, girl!" Nicholas slugged down his beer. "Who else knows that you are pretending to be a law student besides me and Randy?"

"Just a few trustworthy friends." Nina looked around to make sure no reporters were around the booths.

"How about lover boy?" Nicholas asked.

"Yes, he knows," she whispered. "Will you please keep your voice down."

"Then what was that 'where's Nina' bit back at his penthouse? Awesome digs by the way," Randy said.

"Look, I haven't told him that I'm the Nina who went to Haiti with Amandine because he thinks that woman is the key witness in Amandine's case. You see, I can't be one person working on the case and another testifying. He might be accused of trying to fabricate evidence or something. He'd lose his license if they could prove that he knew about it and then chose to call me as a witness."

"So why don't you just tell him all that, and let him decide what to do? He seems cool about all your other lies," Nicholas said.

"You make it sound like I'm this pathological liar who gets my kicks out of this." Her mouth contorted angrily.

Nicholas flashed a superior grin as he raised his beer mug. "You said it, not me, darling."

"It's not funny. I was just trying to get Amandine asylum and no one would help me. But now look, look at all of these refugees being helped. If I hadn't done anything, many would be forced back to Haiti and be severely persecuted. Look, I think I've done a good thing. But as you said Nicholas, I'm in this case too deep right now to reveal the truth."

"I think you're doing a wonderful thing," Randy added. "You should see the refugees. They have such an amazing spirit. I mean, we take so much for granted, like just sitting here having a beer without having to look over our shoulder all the time. They risk their life for this stuff."

"They have beer in Haiti." Nicholas laughed, thrusting his chin forward. "No seriously, Nina you're awesome. Just come clean with your beau before it's too late." He scratched his head. "I wonder how Remmy feels about being this famous law clerk?"

"You're still thinking about her?" Nina asked.

"Sometimes. I may give her a call."

"Good." She smiled sincerely. "I think you're right. I'm going to just tell Steve everything. I'm going to right now." She stood up. "You know. I'm glad I talked to you guys."

She kissed each of them on the cheek and said good-bye.

"I think Nina's in love." She overheard Randy and Nicholas as she walked away.

When she reached the door to the penthouse, it was open so she let herself in. The penthouse was pitch black and silent. Nina tiptoed into the bedroom, removed her clothes and slipped into bed. Then she put her arm across the bed to find Steve. She wanted to curl up in his arms.

"Steve?" Nina whispered to the other side of the bed, but she did not feel his body in the darkness. She reached over and turned on the lamp. He was gone. She went to the living room, calling his name. Moving faster, she searched each room, then she glanced up on the dining room table where Steve had placed the envelope from the photo center. She opened it up and it was empty, except for the negatives. She walked over to the light, holding them up. It was the negatives of the original pictures she had from Haiti. She had never discarded them. They had the pictures of her.

Nina got dressed and left the penthouse to find Steve. She took a subway to McNamara's office at about 2:00 a.m. She had a key and let herself in. She knew it was not safe to be roaming the offices alone at this hour on a Saturday night, but she did not care. She needed to find Steve and talk to him. He would never trust her now.

She scurried through the labyrinth of cubicles and hallways until she came to the library. The table was stacked with law files and casebooks. Nina shoved them to the floor and watched them topple. As their spines cracked against the floor, Nina kicked them with her heel.

When Nina went back to the penthouse, the door was locked and no one answered the door, so she spent the rest of the night stirring in bed in her empty dorm room with her eyes wide open and her arms folded tightly across her chest. She thought about the owner of the photo center's words, "Where have I seen you before?" Nina knew that Steve had the pictures of her.

At around 6:00 a.m., Nina went downstairs to retrieve the paper. She skimmed the headlines and was relieved to find that she was not listed as the key missing witness.

She bought some orange juice and a plain bagel, then headed over to Washington Square Park, the way she used to do on Sunday mornings before she met Steve. She lingered around the park, sporting Steve's aviator sunglasses that she had found in her pocket from the day before. It was a hot August day. She watched hacky sack players, listened to people play guitar and watched some students run through the fountains with their clothes on.

After about an hour, she went over to where the chess players were and sat on the sidelines watching their game. She recognized all of the men. When one of the guys lost. Nina moved in to play.

"Hey it's you, the Russian. I missed ya," Charlie said. His life had remained unchanged over the past year, playing chess in the park every day that the weather was tolerable. Still, she defeated him in only seven moves.

"Still miss me?" she asked.

"Hey, you are my most worthy opponent."

The next day was Monday and Nina had to go into work with her hair pulled up into a straw hat, aviator sunglasses on her face, and a pair of jeans and T-shirt because her Remmy disguise was at Steve's place. She walked swiftly through the halls just waiting for someone to pounce on her about her outfit, and she looked for Steve, but he continued to be miserably absent.

Nina walked into her own office and glanced up at her desk. In the center, next to her computer, was the

177

envelope where the photographs had been. Nina's heart was beating fast as she approached it. She flicked the lid open and peeked. Inside was a little Russian doll.

Nina sat on her desk admiring the Russian doll. She unscrewed the body and pulled out a smaller, wooden doll. Then she unscrewed three more dolls consecutively; the tiniest one was solid.

As Nina sat staring at the dolls, she didn't realize Jim McNamara was standing by her desk looking down at her. He cleared his throat and said, "What are you doing?"

Nina was startled and flinched in her chair. "I was thinking," she said in a quiet voice.

He stared at her straw hat and aviator glasses, taking it in. "I see you are ready for the beach. That's good. Because you're going to Miami tomorrow."

"Tomorrow?"

"Yes. You'll fit right in at the Refugee Clinic with all your causes."

"Tell me, Jim, why are you so against change?"

"I'm not against change. I'm against taking away jobs of Americans and giving them to immigrants."

"This country was started by immigrants."

"So, you can say Adam and Eve were immigrants too, but at some point you have to draw the line."

"And what point is that?"

He looked up in the air, thinking for the first time before shooting off his robotic mouth. "I don't know. I guess it depends on your vantage point. For me, I think we have enough people in this country. I guess my immigrant grandfather may have thought differently."

"Exactly." She waved her hand in the air. "But we should get away from only thinking what is best for our own interests."

"We are helping you, aren't we?"

"Yes. And I'm grateful for your contributions."

He sat in the chair, and leaned forward. "Why are you so concerned about these refugees?"

"I just believe in freedom and democracy. And if someone can't have it in their country, then they should be welcomed here."

"Anyone? Or just those persecuted?" He regarded her quizzically.

"Everyone."

"And where do we put them all?"

"We could start with your great state of Texas."

He smiled in good humor, then stood to his feet. "Have fun in Miami. Don't forget to visit South Beach." He walked towards the door. "Oh, and by the way, there is a student who will be accompanying you on your journey. He's in the library."

Nina stood in the entrance of the library. It was still a mess from her tantrum on Saturday night. But in the middle of the chaos, a familiar head poked through and turned to greet Nina.

She ran to hug him. "Art Levin, what are you doing here?" She felt safe in his scrawny arms. "Gosh, I didn't think anything could make me happy now."

He smiled.

"So what brings you to McNamara & Associates?" she asked.

"What do you think? The refugee cases. Ever since you first told me about them, I've been dreaming about assisting you. Of course I'm not quite a law student, yet, like you." He winked. "But I can do lay person duties."

"Boy am I glad to see you." She pulled a chair next to him.

He looked at her. "Hey, are you okay? Is this the disguise you were telling me about, Remmy?" He elbowed her in the arm and winked, again.

"Sort of."

Nina was delegated to go to the Refugee Clinic in Miami to conduct several interviews of refugees with other law students around the country. Wess Salinger would be overseeing their work and McNamara & Associates would be footing the bill. Nina taught Art the procedure for conducting a worthwhile interview. She explained that she was supposed to get their personal background, where they were when Aristide came in to power and what was their private and public reaction. Did they support him publicly both before and after the coup in September of 1991 and were they ever threatened or abused by the authorities of their country for taking the political side of Aristide. Furthermore, it must be asked how they got here and what the details of their journey were, and were they fleeing for their life. It also must be asked who were their friends and would they agree to be a witness in other refugee cases.

Finally, the students must ask what they thought would happen if the refugee were to return to Haiti.

Art was delegated to be Nina's assistant.

After work, Nina went to Steve's penthouse to retrieve her belongings. She needed her Remmy Peterson costume to go to Miami. She could not very well walk around in sunglasses and a hat around the Detention Center, besides it was a good excuse to stop by. She ached so much to see him. However, when she arrived at the door, the doorman told her that Steve had told him he did not want to be bothered by anybody.

"But I need to get my things. All of my clothes and files, everything is up there," Nina insisted. "Can you at least call him for me and tell him I need my things?"

The doorman shrugged, then called up to Steve's penthouse. Nina was sweating profusely. She thought if she could just see him to find out what exactly was going on, she could explain her position. When the doorman got someone on the line, he handed the receiver to Nina.

"Is it Steve?"

"No, it's some lady. She says she wants to talk to you."

Nina grabbed the phone. "Hello. Who is this?"

"Yvonne Lindell-Frank."

"Yvonne? What are you doing up there? Where's Steve?"

"He went for some dinner."

"With who?" Nina could feel her face get hot.

"With some intern. Louise something."

Nina was silent.

"Look, can you please wait there. I'm coming down."

She came to the lobby in her play clothes. Nina had never before seen the woman without a tie. She told Nina that they had all been working on the cases in the penthouse.

"Did Steve and Louise take the limo?"

"I don't know. I think they just walked somewhere."

"How does he seem?"

"How?" She looked up, fully concentrating on the question, because she treated all questions indiscriminately whether they were about the law or the weather. But Nina liked her enough. Nina thought Frank kind of enjoyed working on these immigration cases. "You know, actually he's been kind of cranky, very serious all of a sudden. He seems to have lost his sense of humor."

They walked into a Greek diner and ordered some coffee. "So what are you working on?" Nina asked.

"Well, Steve had the photographs that his secret witness, Nina Selinsky, sent to him. They are all blown up to 8 X 10's and he also made small slides out of them. They're great. You should see them."

"What did he tell you about the secret witness?"

"I told him that I met her almost a year ago in my office." She poured some skim milk into her coffee, stirring it with a skinny red straw. "You look great by the way, Remmy, you've lost tons of weight, and, you're ready for the beach, I see." She was staring at the hat.

"Well, I'm not exactly going to sport a bikini."

"It's funny you should say that. The pictures of Nina Selinsky and Amandine in Haiti had them sporting around in matching blue bikinis."

"You saw these pictures?"

"Yes. I verified to Steve that the girl in the picture was the same one I met in my office." She scratched her head. "Where to find her, I don't know."

"Steve doesn't know where she is either?"

"That's what he said."

CHAPTER 10

The next morning, Nina took some money out of her savings and bought three new suits in her size. Now that everyone thought she lost weight, she did not need to use the padding anymore. But as for the wig and tinted glasses, they were properly in their place. She arrived at the airport around 10:00 a.m. Art had joined her with an armament of casebooks. Nina plopped down next to him in the waiting area and they reviewed the strategies for the interview process.

Their first witnesses had scheduled appointments for 1:00 p.m. the next day. Nina was responsible for conducting four interviews a day with other students, until all twenty-seven were documented. Then they were supposed to prepare a formal memorandum to

Steve outlining the findings of all the interviews and the relevance they had as witnesses to various cases.

Nina looked over the intakes done on the phone over the past week. They were generally consistent. They were all known supporters of Aristide, all were persecuted for their beliefs in one way or another, all fled the country by boat, all had been arrested and were residing at the Detention Center. Many had known the Dubois family who was at the center of the investigation and many had agreed to serve as a witness on their behalf.

Nina's first client was named Leon Raison. Nina greeted him in the visitors' room, once again, behind a wall of glass, like pheasant instead of a human being.

Nina poured strong Haitian coffee out of a thermos into a Styrofoam cup and asked the translator to ask Leon if he wanted some. When Leon smiled with perfect white teeth, Nina summoned the guard to deliver the cup of coffee to her client. They sat for awhile talking about Leon's background, sipping coffee in between translations. Nina had thought of his face and on so many occasions had been titillated by the memory of his bulging biceps pushing off to shore with his oar, encouraging his passengers with a hopeful song.

In Nina's mind, the image of Mr. Raison's erect, muscular physique, chin slightly tilted towards the direction of possibilities, and eyes laden with unwavering courage became synonymous with the Haitian's pursuit for a better life, and now he was miserably cloistered underneath an oversized orange jumpsuit. Yet the sparkle in his eyes was as alive as ever.

"You look uncomfortable in that uniform. Should I have them get you a smaller size?" Nina asked him.

He shook his head.

The translator said, "The truth is, the night I fled to America, I was only wearing a T-shirt. I didn't bring any other clothes. It's actually nice to feel warm."

"Tell me about the night you came here."

"Which one?" the translator said. "I've come here many times. I'm the boatman, rescuing souls along the way."

Nina moved closer to the window as if he could understand her English better that way. "You mean to tell me, that you risk your life to go back and forth to Haiti?"

"Someone's got to steer the boat. I've got experience."

"You are a martyr."

"Is this a question?" the translator asked.

Nina looked at her. "No. It's a statement."

The translator repeated her words and he smiled, speaking again. "He said that you are a martyr, too, and that he remembers you from Haiti." The translator looked at her. "He said to take off your glasses and wig."

"I don't know what he's talking about. Can you please leave the room for a second?"

The translator rolled her eyes, and exited through the door. Nina felt like she was undressing as she removed her glasses and wig and stepped up to the glass.

Later she read his transcript.

He had worked for the Dubois family, and was Amandine's and Blaise's bodyguard for years. He was a huge supporter for democracy and was the one who had turned them on to the revolutionary ideas. He had introduced them to the underground committee meetings that were taking place in support of Aristide both before he was elected and after the coup in September of 1991. He had always known Arnaud to be a fair man who had treated him well, always giving him fresh produce to take home to his family. He had a wife and seven children still back in Haiti, and plans to go back on his boat to get them whether he is granted asylum or not. He said nothing will keep him from his mission, and as long as there is no freedom in Haiti he will continue to be the boatman. He explained that he is also the one who sets up networks in Miami for the refugees to be housed and get jobs under the table. He takes them to the Refugee Clinic and arranges for them to get supplies and receive free counsel. He was finally busted this summer by the coast guard when he was taking Arnaud and Blaise to Florida. He said now that he is incarcerated, many people from Haiti will not be able to come here and the fisherman, Theron, would be harboring people with nothing but empty promises. He said we must not try to contact Theron because the government may intercede with the mail and their underground network would become exploited. He asked that he be granted parole immediately so he can get his family.

After the week was over, Nina learned that she had been the only witness to the persecutions in Haiti who was not a refugee herself, the only one who had nothing to personally gain by her testimony, the only independent witness.

When interviews were completed. Nina and Art prepared a formal memorandum to Steve. It was the only contact Nina had achieved with Steve all week.

Memorandum

TO: Steve Peterson, esq.
FROM: Nina Pavlova and Art
            Levin
DATE: August 7, 1993
RE: Interviews with
            refugees

Nina Pavlova, along with other law students, have interviewed 27 refugees who have traveled to the States by boat to seek a safe haven from political persecution in Haiti and are pleading for asylum.

Furthermore, the refugees' testimonies about persecutions seem credible and consistent and corroborate each other as to details of committee meetings, raids and persecutions. We will be making recommendations as to which ones would be best suited to take the stand and testily for other asylum applicants. All of the refugees have given us sworn affidavits that can be admitted into evidence.

Finally, not one refugee could think of an independent witness to testify in this case, meaning one that did not have a personal gain in this matter, meaning one that was not a refugee. If you have further questions, you may contact us at the Refugee Clinic.

On Monday morning, August 10, 1993, Nina put on her new olive pantsuit, grabbed the file of affidavits and headed over to the INS. This would be the first encounter she would have with Steve since the night he disappeared with the envelope.

Nina inhaled a deep breath of fresh air and walked with authority into the INS building. She looked up on the docket then proceeded to Courtroom Three where the parole hearing was to be held at 10:00 a.m. for Arnaud Dubois. Currently, Amandine's case had been rescheduled to a later date, in light of the new witnesses who had developed. It was only 9:00 a.m., but Jim McNamara had told her to come an hour early to discuss the possibilities of asking the judge to issue a work card for Arnaud.

As she came in, Steve, Art and Jim McNamara were sitting on the bench outside, engrossed in a discussion. Nina walked towards them cautiously, unsure about Steve.

"Good morning," Art said, walking over to greet Nina. The others quickly nodded in her direction but then continued their discussion. Nina's legs were wobbly as she moved over to the adjacent bench with Art and sat down.

"What's going on?" Nina asked as she looked past Art's shoulder at Steve's back. It was strong and muscular. As Art babbled on about the parole process, Nina remembered a happier time when she had lain in bed curled up next to Steve, massaging that very back.

"Hey, are you listening to me?" Art asked.

"What? Yes. I'm listening. You were saying..."

"I was telling you that a wealthy produce distributor has offered to hire Arnaud to sell fruit at his produce stand and you just sat there, not at all fazed."

"What are you joking?" Nina asked.

McNamara and Steve both looked at Nina, and McNamara put his index finger to his lips to suggest to Nina to be quiet.

Nina walked over to them. "Look, I'm part of this team. I'm the one who started this case and I would appreciate it if I could be let in on what's going on." Nina focused on McNamara as she spoke, she was too nervous to make eye contact with Steve and her voice was quivering.

"Remmy, no one is excluding you. You're the one who sat over there." McNamara pointed to where Art was still sitting. "Look, you've reviewed all of the evidence. We can get Arnaud parole, but he's going to have to show that he can support himself and will not be siphoning money from our taxpayers on the welfare system." He looked at her sideways. "Thanks to much of your work, we have a slam dunk case for asylum." He gestured like he was shooting a basket. Nina ignored him as she stared at the back of Steve.

"Young lady, are you listening to me?"

"Yes, I'm listening. Please, go on," Nina said.

McNamara peered down his nose, then continued. "Well anyway, Steve got here an hour ago to meet with Rudy Fussino, the owner of a produce stand in Boca. Steve told Fussino that Arnaud had produce experience and that he needed a job. Steve convinced him to make the hire and he agreed."

"Arnaud Dubois was the wealthiest man in Haiti."

"So?"

"So he shouldn't be working at a produce stand."

"Why not? He has no other credentials that would be adequate in this country," McNamara said.

Nina gazed at Steve, then spoke to him for the first time. "You did this? You got him a job at a produce stand?"

Steve nodded.

"What happened to the American Dream?" Nina threw her file of affidavits at them and stormed off. No one followed her.

Nina sat in the bathroom stall and cried. She just wanted it all to end, to proceed with her life.

At 10:00 a.m., Nina came out of the bathroom, her eyes bloodshot from crying. Then she took her place behind Steve and McNamara in the courtroom. She was seated next to Art. Nina and Art were not permitted to sit at the counselors' table because they were purportedly just students. But they were in close enough proximity to communicate if it proved necessary.

When the clerk called immigration case A93-2334, Steve stood up to introduce himself and McNamara as counselors representing Arnaud Dubois. Then Jim Swenson stood up on the other side and announced his representation of the INS. Nina could see the INS officers over by the table and tried to think that they had assumed this job to help immigrants, like Randy. But as she had realized in the past few months, who knows where one can end up when embarking on a new journey. She looked at Arnaud. He was in orange prison clothes like a common criminal.

"Your Honor, at this time, on behalf of the INS, we would like to acknowledge that we have reviewed the deportation proceedings, and we would like you to acknowledge that Mr. Dubois has access to much wealth and resources and could easily be a flight risk if granted parole. In short, if we allow him to be discharged from custody, it is likely that Mr. Dubois would secretly integrate into our population and we would never see him again." Swenson looked straight at the judge, averting his eyes from the client table.

Judge Telemacher spoke as he read from a file on his desk. "It is my understanding that Mr. Arnaud Dubois came here on a boat with nothing in his possession." He looked up and glared at Swenson. "Is that correct?"

"Yes, your Honor."

"And how do you respond Mr. Dubois to Mr. Swenson's concerns?" Judge Telemacher asked Arnaud directly. He was a tall, sturdy judge who was a senior in his profession. He liked to look pleaders in the eyes to make them accountable.

Arnaud stood up awkwardly in his jumpsuit. "Your Honor, I have lost all access to wealth in my country upon my decision to flee Haiti in pursuit of political freedom."

The Judge cleared his throat as he looked down at the file. "And you, Mr. Dubois, you understand that if you are granted parole, and then fail to show up for your hearing, you will be deported immediately?"

"Yes, I do."

Nina could hear his voice quivering.

"And do you have anywhere to stay or a way of providing for yourself economically?"

Jim McNamara stood up. "Your Honor, Mr. Dubois has been offered a position with Fussino's produce. At this time we petition the court to issue a work card for Mr. Dubois to support himself pending his asylum hearing."

"I object to this." Swenson stood to his feet.

"Sit down Swenson. Mr. Dubois, do you have anywhere to stay?"

Steve rose to his feet. "My client will be staying with me in my hotel until he has enough money to rent an apartment."

Nina flashed Steve an endearing smile.

"Objection!" Jim Swenson popped up. "An attorney can't harbor an undocumented immigrant."

"Sit down," the Judge said. "He is not illegal at this point. He is under the court's jurisdiction, and counselor can room with anyone he chooses."

"Your Honor with all due respect, this case has been a field day for the press, and I think you're being unduly influenced, on a subconscious level of course," Swenson retorted.

"You're wearing my patience. When this proceeding is finished, I'd like to talk with you in my chambers," Telemacher said.

Jim Swenson plunged back in his chair next to a female INS officer who was dressed in a red suit, chewing a wad of gum.

Then the Judge told Arnaud to take a seat and he addressed Steve. "I presume you have discussed these arrangements with your client?"

Steve rose. His voice was strong. "Yes, your Honor."

"Very well, I will grant parole and the work card."

"Thank you, your Honor," Steve said, smiling triumphantly as he sat back in his chair.

Nina watched as they released Arnaud Dubois into Steve's custody. Nina saw that Arnaud's eyes were brimming with joy.

In the back room of the Refugee Clinic, McNamara, Steve, Art, and Nina sat around the oblong table discussing research and theories. McNamara led the strategy meeting. "All right, basically we have enough resources to handle all of the refugees that the students interviewed. We'll continue to get parole and work cards for the refugees, and try to find them independent places to stay." He eyed Steve. "I don't think you have enough room in your hotel for twenty-seven refugees, do you?"

Steve laughed, demurely, shaking his head. "No, but I'd be happy to take Blaise. His parole hearing is next week."

"I'll take some," Art said.

"Art, you're sleeping on Ziv's couch," Nina said quietly.

"Who's Ziv?" McNamara scrunched up his face.

"An old family friend," Nina said.

"This is getting very personal," McNamara said. "Soon I'll be having refugees in my room."

Everyone laughed, breaking the tension in the air. "That would be kind of touching to see, Jim," Nina said. "I think you're kind of starting to dig these cases."

McNamara continued, "I don't dig anything. Except gold. And after these refugee series are over, I'm going back to..."

"To what?" Nina interrupted. "Once you've stretched your heart to be selfless, it's hard to do anything else."

McNamara was quiet, biting his lip. "So, let's go over Amandine's case. Our first asylum hearing is coming up. Steve, what's going on? Did you find that missing witness?"

He looked at Nina. "No. Unfortunately no."

"Can we win without her?"

"I hope so."

The crew scattered about and Nina watched Steve enter Salinger's empty office. It was the first time Nina had found him alone since the night he disappeared with the envelope. She stole the opportunity and quietly strolled into the office.

"Can I talk to you?" she asked.

He shrugged silently with his body stretched out in a wooden chair and his feet balanced on top of the desk. She sat at the edge of the desk, the corner prodding into the back of her thigh. "Thanks for the Russian doll. It's beautiful," she said in a soft voice.

"Oh, you like it? Good. I thought it was appropriate." He looked at her with an enigmatic expression.

"Why are you so mad at me?"

"You don't know?"

"I guess it's because you found out that I was the key witness in Amandine's case and I didn't tell you."

"You lied to me, Nina. The night I first made love to you, I thought I explained that you were more important to me than any of this, and I just wanted an honest relationship."

She took a deep breath. "I know. But I wanted to protect you."

"From what?"

"Look, I'm the key witness in this case, but I'm also one of the key legal minds. You could get into a lot of trouble if people found out that you knowingly tampered with evidence. I didn't want you to have to choose between doing the legally ethical thing of revealing me as a witness or protecting me." She made large hand gestures as she spoke. "I didn't want you to have to compromise yourself that way."

"But now I've had to, anyway."

"I know and I'm sorry. I really am."

He nodded, then moved to the window that was facing a secluded street in Little Haiti. "Look, I bared my soul to you and told you I loved you. I wanted to have an honest relationship, but you can't have a relationship muddled in lies." He looked at her. "What other lies did you tell, and how many more will there be?"

"None. It's all out in the open now. The only lies I told you had to do with covering the fact that I was the witness."

He sat on the windowsill. "Okay, like what?"

She sat next to him, swinging her feet. "Well, like, the fact that I did find the camera in Haiti, but I couldn't tell you because I didn't want you to see my photograph. So instead, I lied and then sent them to you later from alias Nina Selinsky."

"What else?"

"Well, I didn't really have a rip in my pantyhose that one morning you chased me out of the library." She giggled. "I just wanted you to stop asking questions about when my friend Randy delivered my passport."

"What else?" he said, with his hands covering his eyes.

"The picture of the beautiful woman and little girl in Soloman Horowitz' album was me."

He looked up, smiling. "I knew so." He waved his finger in the air. "In fact, to be honest with you, when I found out you were Nina, I kind of figured the whole thing out. I mean two Ninas, come on." He shook his head. "But, somewhere inside me, I just wanted to trust you."

"But you didn't really. That's why you went sneaking around trying to get the photographs developed." She gave him a long searching look. "So you weren't completely honest with me either."

"As I said, a relationship based on lies." He scrunched up his face. "When I made love to you, it meant something to me."

"And you don't think it meant something to me?"

"I don't know."

"Steve, it was my first time," she said softly.

He touched her arm gently. "Look at me." He lifted up her chin, gazing in her eyes. "Is that true?"

She had tears in her eyes. "Yes. I wanted to save myself for someone I truly loved," she whispered. "And I do Steve. I love you."

He let go of her arm, pacing around. "I love you too, Nina. But I just don't know if I can trust you again." He walked towards the door. "Give me some time."

CHAPTER 11

Judge Louis Weinstein was a jovial fellow with a ruddy complexion and acne. Still, he had a pleasant face, perfectly round with a wide smile that displayed teeth that had undergone years of braces. He had dimples on the sides of his cheeks. He was a young judge, in his early forties.

"It is wonderful to have him," McNamara whispered back to his team as Judge Weinstein proceeded to the bench.

"Is he pro-immigration?" Art asked.

"He used to work in the Refugee Clinic," McNamara said as he made his eyebrows dance around his forehead to show his approval.

The Judge spoke. "Good morning, counselors. On the docket today, we have a motion in Amandine

Dubois' asylum petition. The INS has moved for an immediate hearing date. Does the petitioner have any objection?"

"No objection, your Honor. The petitioner is ready to plead her case now," Steve said.

Judge Weinstein gave a little chuckle and said, "Take your time. This is a serious matter." He reviewed his calendar with a calculating eye, then said, "Hearing is set for Monday, August 31, 1993. Any conflicts?"

"No, your Honor," Steve said.

"No, your Honor," Carl Albright, INS attorney repeated. Weinstein slammed down his gavel and motions were closed.

As they departed the courtroom, McNamara went outside to offer some statements to the press and Albright charged towards Steve.

"So you think you are ready to put on this case now, huh?" Albright mocked. "How long have you been representing immigration cases?" He circled Steve slowly, but Steve remained calm.

"I don't think I've seen your face before these hearings," Albright said as he stuck his face under Steve's prominent chin and looked up. "Well, let me tell you something, I've got heaps of experience." Then he swaggered off to talk to the press.

Nina and Art went to lunch at the bagel shop where Amandine and Remmy both served them bagels and lox and egg creams.

"Hey, remember when we went to eat at the Village Coffee Shop, you were friends with the waitstaff, there, too. You sure make friends wherever you go," Art said.

Nina recalled how he had shouted cheers in the booth when he was going over the LSAT answers in his study book, making her feel nostalgic. "I remember Randy and Nicholas were hovering around our table in a kind of mockery. They were dumbfounded by my new ambition to become a lawyer."

"Well, you're awesome. You have an incredible legal mind. You picked the right profession."

"I haven't exactly picked it. It kind of picked me." She gave a polite laugh. "But you know something?"

He shrugged his shoulders.

"I really love it," Nina said. "I think it's what I was meant to do."

When they finished their lunch, they trailed along a boardwalk over the dunes of Delray, watching children play in the sand. Nina moved to the shore, taking off her shoes and helped a little boy build a sandcastle with his yellow bucket and red shovel.

Art knelt to help, but filled the bucket with dry sand and it failed at cementing the castle.

Nina stuck her feet in the water, then scooped up a thick, wet sand pile and packed it into the bucket then turned it upside down. "Watch." She pulled it up carefully, making a perfect mound, not one grain lost.

The little boy clapped. "More. More."

Nina sat next to Art, unlacing his shoes. "Loosen up. Frolic in the mud."

He laughed, nervously. "You know, when I was little I used to play on this exact beach."

"You did?"

"Yes. My grandmother lived down here. We used to come on the holidays."

"That's really nice," Nina said.

"No, it really wasn't nice. None of the kids would ever play with me and my father was always pressuring me to go over to make friends with the kids, but I was always too shy."

"I don't think you're shy," Nina said. "You approached me that day in the LSAT class and asked me to be your study partner."

"Yes, but you know, that was the first time I've ever done anything like that," Art said. "I would see you come into that class everyday and I would think, I just had to meet you. I would walk by you and try to say something, but nothing would ever come out of my mouth." He played with his bow tie. "I thought someone as beautiful as you wouldn't talk to someone like me."

"Seriously?"

He nodded.

"I think you're very handsome," Nina said. "Really. You just need some confidence." She loosened his tie, taking it off, shaking it out.

"You think so?"

"Yes, I know so. There are plenty of girls out there who would give anything to be your girlfriend."

"And you, what about you?"

"What about me?"

"Would you, you know, ever take interest in me, um you know, in a romantic way?"

Nina studied Art's face. He looked so hopeful. She put her arm around him. "Arty, you're an awesome guy. One of my best friends in fact. But I don't, I don't feel that way about you."

Art nodded slowly, biting his lip. Then looked at her. "Why?"

"I don't know. No one can explain love," Nina said in a quiet voice.

He shuffled his feet, kicking sand here and there. "It's Steve isn't it? You're in love with him."

Nina looked off into the distance. "Yes," she whispered. "I'm so sorry." She put her hand on his chin and looked into his eyes underneath his glasses. He looked wounded.

As Nina rode back to Natasia's condo, she felt sad. Art was such a solid guy, clever and sensitive. She had always revered him as her cerebral guide. Arty never judged Nina, even when she wore belly shirts and pranced around with her black toenails.

On Monday, August 24, 1993, ironically, Nina started her freshman year of law school. She could not believe she was going to have to wade through it again, pretending to be herself. After awhile when one is caught up in a lie, it becomes difficult to discern what is truth. Nina looked at the other students, so eager and fresh, whereas her brain had already been melted down and molded into a lawyer's brain. That was the purpose of first year. Her peers, the second year students, hustled around the halls in suits with briefcases going to and from their jobs.

Art had also packed up his belongings over the weekend to begin Yale. He was sorry he would miss the hearing, but Nina vowed she would phone him every night with the details. She intended on going back to Miami for it.

The first thing Nina did when she entered school was to visit her friend, Professor Lynn Wiley. Of course, Nina entered Wiley's office in her Remmy costume.

"Remmy Peterson," she said as she stood up to greet Nina. "How is the most famous law clerk in New York City?" The women embraced, and then Wiley stood back to examine her.

Nina emitted an obligatory chuckle. She had always wanted to be famous, but not necessarily for being a law clerk and definitely not as Remmy Peterson. "Is that all, Professor, you mean I'm not the most famous law clerk in the country?"

Wiley postured, placing her hands on her hips. "You probably are, come to think of it. Those hearings you are all conducting are just incredible." She gestured for Nina to come in her office and she sat behind her desk.

"I'll never forget your presentation with the pinneys. This case is right up your alley. I knew you'd be a shining star."

Nina beamed. "Oh, and I have you to thank for all of your valuable information. If it weren't for your mentoring, I would not have been prepared to assist with this case," Nina said. "Thank you."

"Yes, and you know I have been following these cases in the papers quite closely," Wiley said. "I remember that you had once asked me how to get photographs into evidence if the photographer was out of the country. It is almost as if you had some kind of premonition that you would be handling these type of cases." Wiley stared at Nina in a way that made her feel like she was being dissected. The woman had a photographic memory and was dangerous to play with.

Nina was quiet.

"Remmy, we won't be seeing each other that much now that you've graduated to your second year. I only teach freshmen and I only have freshmen as research assistants. But I want you to know that you're always welcome to come to my office if you have an issue you'd like to discuss or if you just want to talk."

"I understand. Well. I hope we can still go to lunch once in awhile." Nina gulped.

"Of course," Wiley said.

"So how was your summer?" Nina changed the subject.

"It was peaceful. I rented a home on Fire Island with some friends. Then at the end of July, we went to a rain forest in Costa Rica. It was marvelous." Wiley smiled. "Relatively free summers are definitely a big incentive for being a professor," she explained. "Did you ever consider teaching law? You have the mind for it."

"No, I haven't thought about it. I think I'm just going to take one day at a time." She took a seat in front of Wiley and said, "Um, do you think I can ask you one legal question?"

"Shoot," Wiley said.

"Can an individual who is working on a case testify as a witness?" Nina asked.

"It depends on who the individual is. If the individual is a lawyer, then he will most likely not be allowed to testify as a witness. Lawyers are held to an ethical standard of professionalism and this type of conduct would most likely pose a conflict of interest."

"Okay, what about a law clerk?"

Wiley laughed. "You're never satisfied with an answer. You always have to reach for the next level." She shook her head. "But it's good to be that way. Especially in this profession."

Nina tried not to look impatient as she awaited the answer.

"A law clerk is not held to the same ethical standards as an attorney. A law clerk is not a member of the Bar and cannot be sanctioned or disbarred. So although a law clerk helping with a case may be impeached by the opposite side as a biased witness, there isn't any rule that would hinder a law clerk from testifying."

"Interesting," Nina said. "Thank you. You're always so helpful."

As Nina began walking out the door, Professor Wiley called after her. "Remmy, are you planning on testifying in Amandine Dubois' case?" She looked wary.

"No. I just wanted to know if I could."

"Be careful. Reputations in the legal field are easily destroyed and almost impossible to get back." Wiley warned. Nina thanked her and said she would be back soon to take Wiley to lunch.

Later that day, Nina headed back to her dorm after spending time in the library studying the same subjects she had aced the year before. Though she did not find it boring, because she was able to see new angles and insights the second time around. She had come to love the American legal system because it was flexible, forever bending and evolving to principle.

She greeted Anthony, then picked up her phone messages in her mailbox. There was a message from her mother and one from Steve. He was back in New York.

She went to the phone booth to immediately call him, her backpack was still in hand. He answered on the first ring.

"Hello," he said in a deep voice.

"Hi Steve. This is Nina."

"Nina, I've been looking for you all day."

"You have?" Nina could hear her heart beating.

"Yes, we have the hearing in six and a half days."

"Oh, so that's why you called." Her voice became disgruntled and she plopped in the seat, causing the backpack to slip out of her listless hand onto her toe. "Ah!" she screeched.

"What're you doing? Are you okay?"

"Not really."

"I'm sorry. I'll call you at another time."

"No. No." Nina perked up. "I'm okay. What is it that you need?"

"Well, we have all of the evidence compiled, the order of witnesses to be called and all of those details, but I need someone to go over the legal theories of the case with me," Steve said. "You know, how you used to do with that silly pointer on my blackboard in the living room?"

Nina laughed. "I remember. I'll be over right away."

"Well actually, I'll just meet you over at the office library in an hour if that's all right with you?"

"Why not the penthouse?"

"I don't know. It would be too distracting."

"I see." Nina's throat was tight.

"Look, I've got to run. I'll see you at the library."

Nina went to her room to look for her best suit. Many of her original Remmy suits were still at the penthouse. She knew that Steve had to wake up there and see her stuff strewn all around his place. He had never asked her to come retrieve them so Nina had not pressed the issue. To Nina, this meant that she was somehow still staying there.

Nina arrived at the library and stood in the door watching Steve work. He was a brilliant lawyer. The

Judge was sympathetic to refugees and she knew Steve would win him over with his charm.

Nina quietly took a seat next to him. She wanted to get close enough to smell his scent before he noticed her. After she sat there for a moment, he turned around and jumped reflexively.

"Hey, how long have you been sitting there?"

"Not long. I just enjoy watching you work."

He blushed and stood up to move away from her. Then he handed her the pointer she had used in the penthouse. "Here, I believe this belongs to you."

Nina stood up to write the elements of persecution:

1   well-founded
2   fear
3   persecution
4   political reasons

They went through all the elements, dissecting them one by one.

As Nina watched Steve, she caught herself mesmerized by his dark green eyes, then quickly looked away. She stood up to get a drink from the water fountain. Steve followed after her down the hallway rambling in her ear.

"You see, it's a perfectly air tight legal case, with the photographs, the testimony of Cerise, Leon, her father and brother, and other refugees who knew her, and of course, her testimony and diary. We also have the newspaper articles demonstrating political strife in Haiti." Steve made a semicircle around Nina as she bent over the faucet. "I just wish we had a witness that didn't have a personal motive." He stopped walking for a moment, and put his hand on her waist, pulling her close to him. "One who saw Amandine being chased by the Haitian soldiers, one who was with her. What an experience you went through." He searched her eyes. "I'm sorry you had to go through that. It must have been awful."

Nina gulped down her water. "Steve, let me testify."

He leaned against the wall, thinking. "I don't know what the answer is."

"Well, do you think with the other evidence, we have enough?"

"I do, but it depends on the Judge."

"What if we don't win?"

"Then we walk out of the courtroom, knowing that we did our best."

"But did we do our best? We can't send Amandine back to Haiti."

Steve lightly grabbed Nina's arm as he led her back to the library. He put the pointer in her hand. "Okay, assume the Judge believes all the testimony that Amandine feared for her life when she fled Haiti, that she was a known political dissenter, and she was chased by the military in a country with known political turmoil amidst others she was with whom were arrested. Do you think he'll grant asylum?"

"Definitely!" Nina agreed. "And if asylum is granted in this case, then the others are sure to follow."

"That's right and we will have made a great difference in the lives of dozens of refugees, setting precedent for many more to come."

Nina nodded and smiled.

"Let's go, Counselor."

CHAPTER 12

"Good morning, your Honor. As you know, my name is Steve Peterson and I am here on behalf of Amandine Dubois. First, I'd like to take this time to thank you for giving your time this morning to preside over this important case." Steve paced along the room, looking at the Judge.

"What you're about to see and hear this week will not be pleasant. In fact, I am certain you will be quite saddened by the conditions in Amandine's country." The courtroom was silent except for Steve's voice and a few reporters tapping on their laptops. Nina could hear Steve's shoes brushing back and forth around the courtroom floor. Then he took his place at the lectern for a dramatic pause.

"Freedom, what a refreshing word. Wouldn't the world be such a nicer place if everyone had freedom?" Steve shook his head back and forth, smiling, dreamily. "But your Honor, the fact of the matter is not everyone has freedom. And over the next couple of days, you're going to hear testimony from several people who have yearned for freedom, risked their lives for freedom, and who are willing to put their own lives on the line for other peoples' freedom. You see, freedom is something we take for granted in this country because we ride on the backs of our immigrant forefathers. I ask you today to listen carefully to all of the witnesses testify in an objective manner, and if you do that, then I'm certain you will come to a conclusion that Amandine Dubois believed in freedom and risked her life to pursue it." Steve walked to his lectern and looked as though reading.

"To be granted political asylum, petitioner must prove she has a well-founded fear of persecution," Steve said in a loud voice, then stepped away from the podium. "If we got behind the eyes of any of these refugees we would be certain to taste the fear they have, if forced to return to their tumultuous country. Your Honor, I have looked into the eyes of Amandine Dubois and have seen her fear." He took another dramatic pause. "Yet the court asks for more. So today I will present you with photographs, newspaper clippings, petitioner's diary and testimony that will demonstrate the political strife in Haiti. Furthermore, the evidence will show that Amandine Dubois was a known dissenter of the present government in Haiti and was participating in a political committee meeting when it was raided, and several of her countrymen were arrested in front of her eyes. That day, Amandine was chased by soldiers with machetes and had to hide in a hot, sauna-like compartment of a fisherman's cottage, until she was taken to a flimsy, wooden boat that was headed for the refuge of America. Your Honor, the Dubois family was a prominent, wealthy family in Haiti that could have lived in luxury behind the walls of the Dubois mansion. Yet Amandine Dubois dared to go beyond those walls to reach for freedom. Please, your Honor, don't be the one to send her back. Don't be the one to send her back to an ill fate of severe persecution. Let her reach the American dream of freedom and democracy. I thank you." Nina could hear gasps from the audience. Steve had been stunning. Nina watched him in adoration as he took his seat next to McNamara at the petitioner's table. McNamara sort of patted him on the back, indicating he was impressed.

Next, Albright stood up to deliver his opening statement. He stuffed his fists between the rolls in his sides as he stomped around the courtroom.

"Your Honor, I'm going to keep this short. I know you have your own life to get back to. I don't want to waste any more of your time." He glared at Steve. "Let me just put this case in a small box for you. On the outside, it's wrapped with fancy paper by the petitioner. They have photographs. They have newspaper clippings. They have other refugees telling you how horrible it was in their country. And, they have the fanfare of the media. But you see, your Honor, when you open the fancy box, there is nothing on the inside. It is empty, void of substance." Now Albright walked over to the Judge and eyed him. "You see, there is absolutely no tangible proof, that Amandine, herself, was persecuted by the authorities in her country and further, there is no proof that she will be persecuted if she was to return to her rightful homeland." Albright modulated his voice to conversational tone. "It's the petitioner's burden to prove this. Thank you." He nodded his head and his large body plummeted into his chair.

When opening statements were concluded, Judge Weinstein called a quick recess and Nina followed Steve out in the hallway. "You were wonderful," she told him.

"Yes, I feel pretty good about it. Thanks to your dramatic coaching." He smiled, graciously.

Nina and Steve had spent the whole weekend in the library in New York rehearsing Steve's opening statement before returning to Miami. Nina had offered him tips on how to captivate an audience and how to be dramatic.

"Well, I guess all of my acting classes paid off in some way."

"You'll never go back to the theater?"

"What, and miss all of this real drama?"

Steve looked pensive for a moment, then he said, "You know it's interesting, it seems as though sometimes an unfortunate event can really motivate a person to improve their life. I mean, it is sad that it has to happen that way, but at least you can have a happy ending." He studied Nina, then whispered, "thank you" before they headed back into the courtroom for the first round of witnesses.

"Your Honor, the petitioner calls Ms. Cerise Martin to the stand."

Cerise sauntered towards the witness table. She still had full hair and her face had filled out a bit. Nina thought she looked adorable in her cotton dress. She swore to tell the truth, then sat in the witness chair. She looked tiny as her head protruded from behind the stand.

"Ms. Martin, can you tell the Judge when you first came to know the petitioner, Amandine Dubois?"

"All of my life. We were close friends since we were little girls."

"Was this in Haiti?"

"Yes Port-Au-Prince."

Steve gave her a smile of encouragement to put her at ease. "Ms. Martin, would you say Ms. Dubois had a happy childhood in Haiti?"

Albright jumped up. "Objection, your Honor! How could she know if Ms. Dubois was happy? She can't get inside her head."

"Sustained," Weinstein said. "Please try not to ask questions that conjecture. Stick to the facts."

"Okay, Ms. Martin what kind of household did Amandine grow up in?"

"Oh, very wealthy and luxurious. She had bodyguards and maids. Only attended the best schools in America."

"What kind of schools?"

"Boarding schools, then college. She dreamed of being a doctor for children someday." She slipped out a dreamy smile.

"Did she plan on living in America some day?"

All eyes in the courtroom were staring at Cerise now. "No! Never! She wanted to become a doctor, then come back to her country," she said.

"Did she tell you this?"

Albright jumped up. "Objection! Hearsay!"

"Sustained."

"Did you tell Amandine about the committee meetings that were going on in support of Aristide?"

"No, I never told Amandine about the committee meetings. She is the one who introduced me to the ideas of democracy. She is the one who took me to the committee meetings."

"Okay, did Ms. Dubois ever tell you that she was worried for her safety because she was a known Aristide supporter?"

"Hearsay!"

"Sustained."

Steve brushed his hands through his thick hair. "Did Ms. Dubois ever come in contact with the state's military while attending a secret committee meeting in support of Aristide?"

"Yes."

"And did she see you there?"

"Yes. When the soldiers raided the meeting, some people were arrested and some fled. Those who got away met later at the boats that were headed for America."

Albright swung his arms. His face was fiery red. "Your Honor, please instruct the witness to answer only the question she is asked. Counsel didn't ask her about the boats or soldiers or any of this."

"Very well," Weinstein said. "Ms. Martin, please answer only the question you are asked. And don't volunteer any extra information, okay?"

"Okay," she said, shrugging her shoulders.

Steve continued. "Ms. Martin, did you go on the boat headed for America with Amandine?"

"Yes, I did."

"And what did you and Amandine do when you arrived in Florida?"

"We stayed at a house until we were well enough to go to the Refugee Clinic to seek advice."

"Were you there alone?"

"No. There were many refugees there."

"What did you do there?"

"We nurtured each other to health, helped each other to get on our feet. It was difficult."

Steve introduced some newspaper clippings that showed the conditions that many had to live in when coming to America.

Nina cringed as she looked at the desperate faces of the refugees. "Ms. Martin, are these photographs in the newspaper similar to the conditions you and Amandine first lived in when you came to the States?"

"Objection!" Albright stormed. "What is the relevance of this?"

"Counsel?" Judge Weinstein looked at Steve.

"Your Honor, I'm trying to establish that life in America for these refugees is a hardship, and the only reason they leave their homes, family, and jobs in Haiti is to seek political freedom, not economic freedom."

"We don't need to establish that life in America is hard. We only need to show that the refugees were being persecuted and had to flee for their life." Albright stammered.

"Mr. Peterson, what is it that you're trying to achieve by introducing these clippings?" Weinstein asked.

"I'm trying to establish a chain of evidence that will lead us into the persecution theory." Steve looked at Albright and said, "The persecution that takes place in Haiti."

"Okay, you may continue, but keep it brief."

"Ms. Martin, are these pictures similar to the type of living conditions you and Amandine experienced when you came to the States?"

"Yes they are," she said, wrinkling her nose.

He gathered the clippings. "Your Honor, I'd like to introduce these clippings into evidence, marked as Exhibit A." Steve gave the clippings to the Judge for his review.

"Ms. Martin, were you aware that life would be hard in America when you left Haiti?"

"Yes, I was."

"But you came here anyway?"

"Yes. There wasn't a choice. We would have been arrested and harmed if we stayed in Haiti."

Steve grabbed some photographs from the petitioner's table. "Okay, I need to ask you to identify the refugee in this photograph." He handed them over to Cerise, who was examining the pictures.

"Can we get you some water?" Steve asked.

Cerise shook her head no, thumbing through all of the photographs. She began to cry softly in her hands. "I'm sorry, many of these people were my friends."

Steve grabbed some tissues from Nina and gave them to Cerise. "Look, if you need to take a break, we can continue this later," Steve said, patting her hand.

"No. No. I'm okay."

"All right." He cleared his throat and proceeded. "Cerise, who is the refugee in that picture?" Steve asked carefully as she glanced over it.

"My fiancée," she muttered and Steve retrieved the photo from her. He turned around and offered the photo into evidence. It was marked and delivered to the Judge. Steve let him examine it for a few moments, then faced the Judge while speaking to Cerise.

"Now Cerise, in the picture, your fiancée is being taken somewhere. Do you know what happened to him?"

"He escaped and he found me, and took me to the boats."

"What do you think would have happened if he had not escaped?"

"He was about to be arrested."

"Do you remember anyone trying to harm you or Amandine?"

"Amandine crouched behind the bookshelf. I jumped out the window and ran with my fiancée."

"Where did you run to?"

"To a fisherman's cottage. He took us to the boats."

"What did you do when you got there?"

"I pulled myself onto the boat with the others. I was crying, and Amandine was comforting me." She narrowed her eyes, looking off into the distance. "I was so afraid."

"Did you fear for your life?"

"Yes. We all did. But we knew that coming to America was our only hope."

Steve walked towards Cerise. "What happened next?"

"The trip was difficult. We got seasick from the waves and dehydrated."

"Did you think you would make it?"

"I wasn't sure."

"Why?" Steve asked.

"Because I don't know how to swim, and I was frightened we wouldn't make it into shore."

"Did the boat make it to shore?"

"No."

"What did you do?"

"Amandine and the boatman pulled a wooden log from the boat and she hauled me in while I floated on top of it."

"Your Honor, what is the relevance of this except trying to portray Amandine like some heroine?" Albright got up in his chair.

"You said it, not me," Steve said, smiling.

"Testimony is fine," Weinstein said.

"Ms. Martin, after all you've been through to come to America and as a refugee here in the States, if you had the chance to do it over again, would you have come to the States on that boat?"

She nodded. "Absolutely. The other choice was severe persecution. At least coming to America, there was hope."

Steve tilted his head to the side. "Well, do you still have hope?"

"I do." Her eyes brightened.

Albright was on his toes with his finger in the air, but nothing came out of his mouth.

"Do you think Amandine should be granted political asylum?" Steve asked.

"Objection," Albright yelled, still on his toes. "Ms. Martin is not a legal expert, she can't decide whether someone should or shouldn't get asylum."

"Sustained."

Steve nodded. "Very well. Your Honor, at this time I submit Ms. Cerise Martin's entire testimony as an affidavit into evidence to be used in this case and future asylum cases that we will be representing."

The Judge nodded.

"I'm so sorry Cerise that you and your people have to go through this." Steve's voice was soft, and he handed Cerise some more tissues.

"Counsel, do you have any more questions?" Weinstein asked.

Steve shook his head. "No, your Honor."

Albright stood and swaggered over to Cerise. He circled her from the front. "Ms. Martin, did you ever see Amandine Dubois being harmed by the military in Haiti?"

"No, I did not."

"Did you ever hear anyone say they were going to harm or arrest Ms. Dubois?"

"No."

"Did Amandine Dubois ever tell you that any soldiers had harmed her or arrested her?"

"No, but they came after her with machetes after the committee meeting."

"Answer only the question." He sneered. "Do you think that you could look the Judge in the eyes and tell him for certain that Amandine Dubois was harmed or arrested by the military of Haiti?"

Cerise shrugged.

"I can't hear an answer Ms. Martin. Shrugs don't get translated into our legal transcripts. Please give an audible answer." Albright gestured with his hand to his mouth to demonstrate where the sound should come from, then rolled his eyes.

Cerise turned to the Judge. "I don't remember what he asked me."

The Judge tapped his fingers on his bench. "Repeat the question, please."

Albright paced around the witness stand and stuck his face close to Cerise. "I asked you if you knew for certain that Amandine Dubois had been either harmed or arrested by the military." He said it slowly like a schoolteacher to a child, then waited for an answer with his hands on his hips.

Cerise made a fist with her hands and put it to her mouth. Her eyes looked towards Nina and she said, "No."

"Thank you. I have no further questions." Albright stuffed his hands in his large love handles as he slowly walked back to the INS table. He showed a toothy smile.

"Rebuttal?" Judge Weinstein looked at Steve. Steve turned to Nina who slipped him notes. He quickly glanced at them and jumped up.

"Ms. Martin, did you ever see an officer of the military of Haiti try to harm or arrest Amandine?" He emphasized the word try.

"They tried to arrest everyone that was at the committee meeting. But Amandine got away."

"So you may not have seen her being harmed or arrested, but you saw them try to harm or arrest her?"

"In the group, yes."

"I have no further questions," Steve said.

"I have one," Albright said, standing to his feet. "Will Amandine Dubois serve as a witness in your asylum case?"

She nodded.

Throughout the course of the week, several more refugees testified in a similar manner. Arnaud was the final witness at the end of the week, and Amandine was scheduled to be the last to testify.

CHAPTER 13

Although he looked much older than the photo, Nina knew he was her father because of his large, smoky blue eyes. Nina had inherited those eyes. He was a young man with premature white hair and a look of distrust. Nina figured this must be from years of living under the Soviet regime, but also from being abandoned by his wife and only child.

Natasia's timing was always inept. Nina donned her best suit for the final round of testimony in Amandine's case, and just as she was descending the staircase of the condo, Remmy greeted her on the third stair to forewarn her that her mother was in the clubhouse with a man. Nina panicked, throwing off her wig and glasses, and letting her hair drape around her shoulders. She was already late and Steve needed her support, but she went back into the condo to fix her hair and apply make-up. When she entered the lobby of the clubhouse, standing next to her mother, looking elegant and auspicious, was the man. He had a white head, and when he turned, Nina knew it was her father, Ivan.

She moved over to the pair cautiously, flashing a demure smile.

Natasia embraced her and said. "It is time to see your father."

Nina gazed at him, her eyes dancing. She had lived this moment in a number of girlish fantasies. But now that it was happening, she was not sure what to do. Ivan stole the burden from her as he scooped her in his arms. Nina buried her face into his wooly sweater, overdressed for Florida, and listened to him.

"Mother, what, what did he say?"

Natasia was sniffling. "He said, you are so beautiful, just like your mother."

Nina called the clinic and told Wess to inform Steve that she would not be at the hearing today.

The Pavlovas strolled along South Beach. It was a fine day, the first of September when the Florida sun is still in full bloom. Under several trees, young people were singing and playing guitar, others rap danced to a loud radio and some were running around with video cameras, making movies of their friends. Youths wove through the crowds on skateboards trying to jump ramps and one man stood near a fountain, speaking about morality and politics.

Ivan's mouth gasped while he digested the scene around him. He spoke some Russian to Natasia as the three of them sat on the bench to eat some bagels.

"What is he saying?" Nina asked Natasia, interrupting their conversation.

Natasia laughed. "He wants to know if all this is what I left him for?"

Nina looked at Ivan. He seemed uncomfortable in this environment. She looked around for a place he could enjoy, then fixed her eyes on a few people playing chess. "Hey, isn't my father the one who taught me about chess?"

"He sure is."

Ivan and Nina settled under a tree near the chess players. It was still early enough on a Monday morning that there was not a large crowd. Well, if Nina could not articulate her thoughts in words, she found a perfect communication across the chess table with her father.

Natasia sat on the sidelines, watching intensely.

They played for an hour, each winning a few rounds, but it was Ivan who tallied the most checkmates. Around 11:00 a.m., Nina left the table for her father to play with a man who wanted to challenge him, and she found her way over to the bench by her mother.

"Look at him, he's so brilliant and dapper. Why did he never achieve success?" Nina asked her mother.

Natasia sat quietly for a moment until she spoke. "It depends what you think of success. In Russia there was not the same opportunities as there are here." She brushed Nina's hair away from her forehead and looked at her face. "You think in Soviet Russia, a little girl like you with no money or connections, could be attending law school?"

Nina smiled, modestly.

"You are very blessed. You should be thankful that I brought you here. I hope some day your father understands and can forgive me."

"But he is here with you now."

"Yes, because we love each other," she said. "He has wanted to come here so badly, and now with all of the changes in Russia, he has finally been able to." Natasia looked at Nina. "You know, Mr. Horowitz cannot do his immigration papers. He is retired."

"I know."

Natasia narrowed her eyes to examine Nina. "How do you know?"

"I went to visit him in my last year of college. He's the one who inspired me to go to law school."

"Really?"

Nina nodded.

"He's a good man."

"You know, I want to do the immigration papers," Nina said.

Natasia looked surprised. "How can you?"

"I'm studying law. Remember?"

"It is just so hard to believe. I mean, to me, you are just my little Nina."

"If he wants to stay, I'm going to do his papers." Nina leaned close to her mother. "Do you think he really wants to stay?"

"He wants to stay."

"With you in Florida?"

"Of course, where else would he stay?"

"So are you happy?"

Natasia looked at Nina and rested her arm around her. "You know, it is funny, you don't see someone for fifteen years, it is hard to learn each other all over again." Natasia smiled. "You see, I have to learn things again, like, how he takes his coffee, his eggs, that kind of thing." She took a tissue out of her purse to wipe her eyes. "But we had a lot of love between us. That has never gone away," Natasia said softly. "What I did, I did for you. I wanted my little Nina to have a better life."

Nina treated her parents to lunch at the bagel shop where Remmy and Amandine worked. Remmy waited on them, articulating the choices of whitefish or chubs.

"Shouldn't you be starting second year law school?" Nina whispered to her.

"I'm withdrawing as soon as you give me the green light."

"I thought you were transferring?"

"Nope."

"So what are you going to do?"

She looked at Nina's father. "Well, now that your father's here, Amandine and I are sort of being kicked out." She winked at Ivan. "Cute dad." She picked up a tray, balancing it with ease on her flat palm. "It's time we get our own apartment anyway. We're looking at condos in Boca."

"And you're just going to work here?"

"I like it. And don't forget my important spy mission of delivering supplies to the refugees," she whispered. "Nina, I finally have a purpose in life. I am happy. Oh, and Nicholas called. He's going to visit me soon."

"Take it slow. No Vegas." Nina waved her finger.

"Well, I don't exactly have the bucks anymore."

"What about your trust fund?"

"Oh that? Yes well, daddy decided I'm still gonna get it when I'm twenty-five."

"Of course."

After the bagel shop, they visited Little Haiti where Nina introduced them to her friends at a coffee bar where they made very strong Haitian coffee. They got double shots, then walked around downtown. She felt moved as she watched her Russian parents promenade, hand in hand. They were talking fast to each other in Russian, laughing and smiling. This was all Nina had ever hoped for since she was a child and she became filled with a serene inner happiness that made her feel whole. Momentarily, she had even forgotten about the hearing. On the docket today, Steve was questioning Blaise about taking the photographs, and laying the foundation for them to all be submitted into evidence.

Downtown, Nina led her parents to a foreign film theater where they saw a movie with subtitles because Ivan could read a bit of English. They shared a bucket of popcorn and Ivan chewed noisily.

The plot was about a young artist who was in love with a girl from a prominent family. The girl had to choose between living her privileged life with a wealthy businessman or marrying her true love, the artist. After much consideration, and various plot lines, the girl, of course, chooses the artist. When the couple kissed at the end of the movie, Ivan stood up and yelled in Russian while clapping his hands enthusiastically. Nina sank into her chair and looked around to see if anyone was watching. Natasia was giggling.

"I guess he likes the movie," Nina whispered to her mother. "What is he yelling about?"

"Oh, just stuff like, how true love can surpass any boundaries."

"Oh, he really gets into it."

"Well, you know Nina, he doesn't go to movies that often in Russia."

Steve was sitting in the lobby of the clubhouse on top of the desk, next to Remmy. He was in a three-piece navy suit, and was swinging his polished shoes back and forth. Remmy was sipping a chocolate Slim-Fast and eating french-fries, while talking continuously. As Nina approached the door, Steve leaped up and ran to her.

He placed his hands on the sides of her arms. "Nina, where've you been?"

"Um, actually, I was at the movies." she said.

"You were at the movies?"

Nina nodded her head yes.

"You mean to tell me that you turned the practice of law on its head with these refugee hearings, you get me out there in the trenches working my heart out and you were at the movies?" Then he veered his eyes towards

231

Natasia and Ivan. They stared at him. He removed his hands from her arms, backed up a bit and smiled, nervously. "Are those your parents?" He whispered.

"Yes," Nina said.

Steve moved towards them to introduce himself. He gave Ivan a firm handshake and Natasia a little hug. Nina's parents conversed in Russian back and forth, sounding a bit frantic. Ivan was swinging his arms.

"What is he saying?" Steve asked Nina.

"How should I know? I don't speak Russian," Nina told him.

He pulled her aside and whispered, "Why didn't you tell me your father was coming?"

"I didn't know. He just sort of showed up this morning. I'm sorry I missed the hearing, but..."

"No, no need to apologize. I'm just glad you're okay," he whispered. "I was really worried about you. I hope you'll come to the hearing tomorrow. I need you there."

Nina smiled, modestly. "You don't need me. You're brilliant all by yourself."

"No, I need you to be there," he said.

"I'll be there. I promise."

Steve hailed a limo and invited the Pavlovas to join him. Natasia and Ivan were still a bit bewildered, but followed the handsome young lawyer into his limo.

He treated them to dinner, and afterwards, the four of them spent the rest of the evening in a Russian nightclub. Natasia was in the center of the floor, spinning on her toes. Ivan held the tips of her fingers as he relished in her sleek movements. Nina and Steve stood on the periphery of the dance floor, watching.

"Your parents are really cool. I never met anyone's parents who went wild at nightclubs," Steve said to Nina as he took tiny sips of vodka out of his glass.

"You're supposed to drink it like this," Nina said, picking up his glass of vodka and swallowing it down in one gulp.

"Wow!" Steve said, staring at Nina.

Nina ordered him another shot. He put it to his lips, threw his head back and swallowed it down. He grimaced and held his lips tight together. Nina doubled over with laughter.

His face turned red, but then he started laughing too. "We come from such different backgrounds!"

"I know." She ran her fingers through his hair. "So?"

He smiled, swaying to the music.

By the end of the evening, Steve bonded with Ivan by doing shots of vodka at the bar. After a few, Steve swept Natasia onto the dance floor and dipped her back gracefully like a swan. Nina and Ivan clapped and cheered them on under the flashing lights and pulsating music.

At 7:00 a.m., Nina's alarm clock buzzed furiously. Her parents were snuggling on Natasia's bed, Amandine was staying at Pierre's place, Remmy was on the couch and Nina was wrapped up in a blanket on the floor. At the sound of the alarm, Ivan jumped up and was bellowing in Russian. Natasia shut it off, then came out into the living room and looked at Nina with her hands on her hips. "What are you doing up so early?"

"Early? I've got to get to court. I promised Steve I would be there at 8:00," Nina said. She took a shower, got dressed and kissed her parents, good-bye. "I'll see you tonight."

Nina heard them conversing in Russian.

"Oh, and your father says to make sure you bring that Steve over again."

"We'll see," Nina said, blowing them a kiss.

She took a city bus, then sprinted through the streets of Miami, her briefcase so heavy, she had to carry it with both hands. It was stuffed with legal flies, aspirin and her red wig and glasses.

CHAPTER 14

"Petitioner calls Leon Raison to the stand," Steve said in a loud voice and the boatman walked to the stand. He had been paroled and the rumor was that he had brought his family back to the States. He was sworn in before he was seated. He stated his name, address and occupation for the record with the help of a translator. All of his testimony was through translation.

Steve paced back and forth. "Mr. Raison, how long have you known Amandine Dubois?"

Translator: "I met Amandine when she was ten years old."

"And how did you meet her?"

Translator: "Let's see." He paused for a moment. "Well, she came into her father's house, drinking a soda. She had on blue jeans and had just taken a walk on the beach before sunset." He laughed, deeply. "She was such a teenager. She didn't want a bodyguard, but her father insisted. She trotted around the house in bare feet, doing a dance like this." He stood up in his chair and wiggled his hips.

Some from the courtroom chuckled. Steve tugged at his cheeks to stifle his obvious grin.

"So why did Arnaud want a bodyguard for Amandine?"

Raison sat back down in his chair. Translator: "They were a very wealthy family and Amandine was quite the little adventurer. She liked to consort with us, commoners." He smiled, displaying his perfect white teeth.

"How do you know this?"

Translator: "Because the arrangement I had with Arnaud was to follow Amandine everywhere."

"What kind of places did you follow her to?"

Translator: "Well, when she was younger I would go to teen parties. That was fun." He laughed. "When she got older, she became more serious. I followed her to many political meetings."

"Were the meetings in violation of the present government?"

Translator: "Yes, Sir."

Steve handed him the photographs that had already been introduced into evidence, then approached the witness stand. "Do you know any of these people?"

He thumbed through the photos.

Translator: "Sure. Everyone of them," he said with a confident smile, arms folded across his chest.

"Did you bring any of these people to America?"

Translator: "Some. Some were arrested by those...." The translator looked at the Judge. "I don't think I can say this word."

"Please don't," Albright said. "No obscenities in the courtroom."

Steve laughed sardonically.

"What is so funny, Mr. Peterson?" Weinstein asked.

Steve paused. "We are surrounded by material of persecutions, that to me are obscene, but Counselor isn't at all disgusted by this. No, he would purportedly be disgusted by a bad word, instead." Steve gestured towards Albright.

Weinstein turned to Raison. "I like clean language in this courtroom."

When that was translated, Raison nodded, saluting the Judge.

Steve walked towards the witness stand. "Mr. Raison, did Amandine Dubois fear for her life when she fled Haiti?"

"Objection your Honor!" Albright jumped out of his chair. "He can't get in her mind."

Weinstein shook his finger at Steve. "Look, Peterson, just ask factual questions."

Steve apologized, then grabbed a newspaper clipping of men on a wooden boat from Haiti. "Mr. Raison, is this like the boat that you traveled on to the States?" Steve asked him, handing him the clipping.

Raison raised his voice, pointing to the clipping. Translator: "That's my boat. Those guys took it." He folded his arms. "It's okay though. I'm happy to help."

Albright rose to his feet. "Your Honor, strike that comment. Strike that comment." He pointed his finger at Raison. "And please instruct this witness to answer only what he is asked. Apparently, Mr. Peterson did not go over the rules with his witness."

Weinstein looked down his nose through his glasses and cleared his throat. "Mr. Raison, you're to only answer the questions asked and nothing more. Okay?"

When it was translated, Raison nodded.

After Steve offered the clipping into evidence, it was Albright's turn to question the witness.

"Mr. Raison, did you ever see Amandine being harmed or arrested by the military in Haiti?"

Translator: "No."

"Did anyone tell you they wanted to arrest or harm Amandine?"

Translator: "No."

"So you have no real evidence that Amandine was harmed or arrested by the Haitian police?"

Translator: "No, I don't have any evidence about anything. I left it behind when we fled Haiti. We don't take anything with us when we are fleeing for our lives."

"So if we told you that the photographs admitted into evidence do not show Amandine being harmed or arrested, what would you say?"

"Objection, your Honor. This question is compound and confusing."

"Shorten it up," Weinstein said.

"Mr. Raison, is it possible that Amandine was spared from persecution because she had a very rich father who was friends with the government?"

"Objection! Your Honor, he is asking an opinion, not a fact. This isn't admissible!" Steve raised his voice.

"Albright, you know better than this. Shorten up the question and ask him only what he has witnessed." Weinstein was stern.

"Mr. Raison, do you know for certain that Amandine Dubois was harmed or arrested?"

Raison thought for a moment, then looked over at Steve, shrugging his shoulders. Translator: "No I guess I don't."

"Mr. Raison, do you plan on having Amandine Dubois testify as a witness in your asylum case?"

Translator: "I don't know."

The Judge called for a short recess and Nina followed Steve out into the hallway.

"I can't stand it when he asks that last question. He asks it every time if the person is going to have Amandine as a witness. Why does he do that?" Steve was breathless.

"Obviously, to leave the Judge with the thought that these witnesses are biased because they have a personal interest, just like we always said." She explained. "Look, I thought you did great. Your objections were right on. You kept him from all of his tricks."

"Yes, but tricks and drama, none of that matters now. He's making a big deal that Amandine was not actually harmed by the Haitian military."

"Because that's all he has."

Steve sat down on the bench, rubbing his fingers through his hair. Nina offered him some aspirin and he swallowed them down without water.

"Rough night?" Nina asked, grinning.

"I had a great night," Steve said, searching Nina's eyes.

Nina sat down next to him. "Amandine is going to testify that soldiers came after her with machetes, that she had to crawl out of a window and be hidden in a secret compartment to save her life."

"Yes, but she's the only one to testify about that. It's just going to be a judgment call by the Judge."

"And what do you think about the Judge?"

"I'm not getting a feel for him. I think he's disgusted about the atrocities in Haiti. But when it comes time to examine the evidence, at this point, we can't corroborate Amandine's testimony that she was chased by soldiers and had to flee for her life, because the only two people who witnessed that, were you and Amandine."

"And Theron, the fisherman."

"Go get him." He flung open the door to go back to the courtroom.

Steve spent the remainder of the afternoon conducting a methodical question and answer session with the petitioner, Amandine Dubois. She was the first to tell the Judge how she had been chased by soldiers with machetes, hid in a secret compartment and forced to flee for her life. The courtroom was silent as Amandine put forth the details of her story. It was the details that were needed for an effective asylum claim. But when Steve was finished, Albright stood up to question the petitioner.

"Ms. Dubois, you and your legal team have put on quite a show this past week." He strolled around her. "But Ms. Dubois, there isn't a witness here who can attest to the fact that you, personally, were chased by soldiers. Why is that?"

"Because, none of these witnesses were with me when I was being chased. They only saw me at the meeting, but they all fled themselves."

Albright rubbed his chin. "So is it your testimony that you were alone when you fled from these military people?"

Amandine stared at Nina. Nina shook her head.

"No. I was not alone."

"Well then who was with you?"

"A friend of mine, Nina. Nina Pavlova."

Steve grabbed Nina's hand under the table and squeezed it.

"Nina, I take it she is not a Haitian?"

There were laughs.

"That is correct," Amandine said.

"So, where is this Nina? Is Peterson going to pull her out of a magic hat?"

"Yes, he is." Nina jumped up out of her seat, all eyes in the courtroom, gazing in her direction, as she approached the witness stand. "I am Nina Pavlova." She took off her wig and glasses and threw them onto the ground.

There were gasps from the crowd.

"Your Honor, what's going on here?" Albright bellowed. "I haven't been informed about this. The petitioner can't just pull out a surprise witness from the audience. This isn't television. We have rules. The petitioner can only call a witness that is on the witness list."

"Nina is on the original witness list," Steve said. "We mistakenly thought her name was Nina Selinsky." He handed the witness list to the Judge.

The Judge reviewed it, showing it to Albright, then waved his finger for Steve to come forward. "Counselor, what's this about?"

"Um, yes, your Honor." Steve pointed towards Nina. "I would like to verify that this is Nina Pavlova, our key witness in this case."

Gasps and pandemonium rippled throughout the courtroom. The Judge slammed his gavel ferociously. But before he could speak, Albright went to Steve's side and pointed his crooked finger in his face. "Of all the dirty tricks I've ever seen attorneys play, this is the worst. We're going to have the petitioner's key law clerk pretend she's the missing witness in this case?" Albright's fists were bunched. "Your Honor, I'd like to request sanctions against Mr. Peterson for this kind of conduct!"

Judge Weinstein removed his glasses again. They appeared to have fogged over by the steam rising in the courtroom. He set them aside, then folded his arms across his chest. "Peterson, I've had it. What on earth is going on here?" he asked in a severe tone.

Steve covered his eyes, almost as in meditation. Then he pointed to Nina and breathed for air. "Your Honor, I promise you on my law license that this is Nina Pavlova and she was in Haiti with Amandine the night of the raid."

"Do you have any proof of this?" Judge Weinstein asked.

Steve took out the photographs of Nina and Amandine in Haiti on the beach and at the committee meeting, and gave it to the Judge. He gave a stealthy glance at the photographs, nodding his head.

"Can anyone else attest to the fact that this is not Remmy Peterson, but rather, Nina Pavlova?"

Remmy pulled her hand from the chewing gum that was wrapped around her finger and slowly rose to her feet with a look of chagrin. She came forward and stood next to Steve. "I can."

"And who are you?" the Judge asked.

"The real Remmy Peterson."

There were gasps and shouting among the audience, and Weinstein had to bang his gavel at least ten times.

"Your Honor, I request permission to question this witness," Steve said.

"I object your Honor! This witness is the petitioner's leading law clerk. She has an interest in the outcome of this case. She has worked on and investigated in this legal proceeding. Under the rules of professional responsibility, an advocate is not allowed to testify as a witness in her own case."

Steve was frozen so Nina addressed the Judge, remembering what Professor Wiley had told her. "Your Honor, with all due respect, I do not have to comply with the rules of professional responsibility, I am not yet a member of the Bar."

Judge Weinstein scratched his chin pensively. "This case has been most unusual. And to be honest with you, I believe that the petitioner has more than put on a sufficient case without this witness." He smiled at Steve for the first time. "You see, the testimony of the petitioner may have been enough to prove fear of persecution, but I appreciate your zealous campaign for such an important issue." Then to Albright, "And you, I don't know what you're trying to do here, but this is not a criminal trial. I've never seen so many objections and manipulations as I've seen from you during this hearing. Why don't you save your quest for fame in someone else's courtroom? I'm not interested in your fancy game. I'm only interested in whether the petitioner would be in danger if she went back to Haiti. So please sit down, and let's hear from this important witness."

Albright reluctantly plopped down in his chair. Nina could see his fingers tapping against the table as she was sworn in.

"Ms. Pavlova, can you tell me when you first met the petitioner, Amandine Dubois?" Steve asked.

"Yes. It was September of 1989. She was my roommate at NYU. We became best friends." Nina spoke slowly, smiling at Amandine.

"Did Ms. Dubois take you to Haiti?"

"Yes."

"Were you informed that you could be in danger upon entering the country?"

"Absolutely not. We were promised protection and had bodyguards to and from her father's mansion. We were supposed to stay within the walls of his home and beach property."

"Had you any idea you would be going to a committee meeting in support of Aristide?"

"Of course not."

"Did you go to a committee meeting with Amandine?"

"Yes."

"Was it raided by the police?"

"Yes, Amandine's brother, Blaise, pulled us behind the bookshelf, and we could hear the screams of the people being arrested."

"Then what happened, Ms. Pavlova?"

"When the crowd dispersed, Blaise came back in the schoolhouse with a soldier. He said the soldier said that the military knew that Amandine was at the meeting and they would be after her. He told us we needed to hide, then took us to their cousin's house. It was there that soldiers came busting through the door with machetes looking for her."

Nina told the whole story about how they had climbed out the window, were chased along the beach until they fled to Theron's cottage and he hid them in his compartment.

"How did you feel?"

"I felt afraid for my own life and I wasn't even the one they were after." She glanced at the Judge. He was intensely listening.

"What did you do?"

"The fisherman took us to the boats and I waved good-bye to my friend, not knowing if I would ever see her again." Nina wiped tears away from her eyes. "Then I went to the airport since they weren't after me, and from that moment forward, I did everything in my power to help my friend, including pretending I was Remmy Peterson the law student."

The courtroom was chaotic. The reporters were tapping away and Albright looked like he was in a trance, shaking his head back and forth.

"Look, I know what I did was wrong and I'm so sorry for all of the people I deceived." She looked into the crowd, scanning the faces of Wess Salinger, Jim McNamara, and Steve. "But if what I did will help Amandine," she looked at Cerise, "and all of the other beautiful people from Haiti, to have a life here away from fear, then I would do it again." She looked at the Judge. "And just for the record, Steve Peterson had nothing to do with me pretending to be his sister. And when he found out, he was professional enough to not call me as a witness so as not to tamper with the evidence in any way."

The Judge was scrunching up his face, squinting his eyes, taking it all in. "You mean to tell me that you did all this just to help your friend?"

"Yes."

"Well Ms. Pavlova, the world could use more friends like you."

CHAPTER 15

Nina flew back to New York that night; it would be her last plane trip on McNamara's bill. He had thanked her, surprisingly, for all she had done, but told her that he could not keep her at the law firm. While there, she made her rounds saying good-bye to all of her friends, Randy and Nicholas, The Horowitzes, Professor Wiley, Yvonne-Lindell Frank, Marcy Weiner, Anthony and Charlie in the park. Her last day, she walked around the city, taking in her favorite sites, saying good-bye to all the homeless people she had become familiar with, dropping coins into their cups one last time.

It was Randy and Nicholas who had been her faithful friends, staying with her until the very end, even drinking a final beer together at "The Sticky Suds" and then, they helped her carry her stuff down from her dorm and loaded it into the trunk of a taxi. "Are you sure this is what you want?" Nicholas asked.

She gulped in some air as tears swelled up in her eyes. "What choice do I have? I've been expelled from law school." Her voice was shaky. She gave him a long hug, then turned to Randy. "And I think I'll miss you most of all." They shut the door behind her, and as the cab pulled away, she watched them get smaller and smaller.

The next morning, Nina woke up and looked out the window. She could see nothing, but highway and trees zipping past her eyes. The bus window felt cold against her ear. She had forgotten her pillow. The man next to her had his chin pointed up and his mouth wide opened. Nina could smell the odor of morning breath.

An hour later, the bus pulled into a truck stop in Richmond, Virginia. The bus driver, a tiny woman, stood in the front aisle. "All right folks, let's get us some breakfast."

The crowd piled out the door and people raced to find a table by the window. Nina hopped onto a stool at the countertop corner. She ordered eggs, grits and black coffee. She saw people reading the papers. She averted her eyes in the other direction underneath dark sunglasses.

"Ja hear?" She heard a woman tell the waitress. "The law clerk was the missing witness, Nina somethin."

Nina slouched in her stool and tried to cover her ears, but she could still hear them.

Erica Axelrod

"Ya know, they're sayin that she and Peterson are an item," the waitress said.

"Well who can blame her?" The woman responded, laughing and smoking.

Nina stopped eating and went back on the bus. She found an empty seat in the back and she squeezed in, crying softly.

The next day, Nina got off the bus in Delray Beach. She bought a newspaper from the cashier at the station and stuffed it in her suitcase without looking at it. Then she took a cab to the beach and sat on her suitcase, staring at the ocean. She could feel the salt in her face and hair. She took her shoes off, running her feet through the sand while she kept her eyes closed, feeling the cold sand grains rubbing the skin between her toes.

She sat there for awhile, mesmerized as the tide rumbled in and then rolled back again. She opened the suitcase to retrieve the paper.

"Asylum granted!" was the headline. Nina stood up and stretched her arms to the sky. Then she ran to the sea, jubilantly skipping through the shallow water and picking up seashells along the way.

Nina slept until eleven in the morning then awoke to the smell of homemade bread.

"Since when do you bake bread?" Nina asked her mother.

"Since they invented bread makers."

Ivan was slicing the loaf with a sharp knife. He cut a piece for Nina and smiled lovingly as she took a bite. They sat at a small table in the kitchen, sipping coffee. Ivan was reading the Moscow News and Natasia was reading the local paper.

"Ha!" Natasia yelled out.

"What now?" Nina asked.

It had been three weeks since Amandine's hearing was over, and she was engaged to Pierre, still working at the bagel shop and getting ready to go back to school in the spring semester.

"You must hear this." Natasia looked down at the paper, reading. "Steve Peterson has went back to his firm that his grandfather started."

"That can't be."

"Yes. It says he is heading up a new department involving refugee work. All refugees, not just Haitians."

"Is he going to be positioned in New York?"

"No. He's going to be working here in Miami with Wess Salinger, partnering with him at the Refugee Clinic."

"He's going to live in Miami?"

Natasia smiled, happily.

Nina walked into the Refugee Clinic for the first time without her wig and glasses.

"We don't accept first year law students," Wess said. "Because we don't know what kind of work they can do." He was in the lobby, grinning at Nina.

"I'll ace the exams," she said, walking towards him. "That's if I was a law student."

"Oh, but you can be." He walked over to her, putting his arm around her shoulders. "I'm on the Board of Admissions at Miami Law School. I've already talked with the other members and they are impressed with your work and courage. They want you to attend their school. An immediate transfer." He led her to his office and shut the door.

Nina had tears in her eyes. "You are kidding."

"No. We need you here, Nina. Between McNamara & Associates and Peterson & Peterson, we have enough funding to hire you as an intern. Arnaud and Blaise will be working with you as paralegals."

"You're kidding."

"No. In fact my new partner demands that we pay you a pretty nice salary."

Nina sat in a cubicle in the Miami Law Library, studying the Federal Rules of Civil Procedure.

"Don't you know all this stuff already?" She heard a familiar voice.

She breathed in deeply, inhaling his wonderful scent. Her heart pounded as she saw his hand place her Russian Doll on top of her book. "I believe this belongs to you."

"I thought I lost this." She stared at the light blue body and blonde hair that surrounded the face. "Thank you. It's beautiful."

She could feel him put his hands on her shoulders and closed her eyes, shivering from his touch. Then he kissed her head and whispered, "Beautiful, just like you, my little Russian Doll."

ABOUT THE AUTHOR

Erica Axelrod graduated with a major in English Literature from Penn State University, then received a Juris Doctorate from the University of Pittsburgh School of Law. While in law school, she attended the Detention Center in Miami and helped Haitian refugees seek asylum. She passed the Bar in Pennsylvania and Nevada and practiced immigration law and housing law in Las Vegas. Her passion in the law has been to help refugees and low-income clients in a legal services organization. However, when she had her first child, she decided to be a stay-at-home mom, and now loves spending time with her husband and three children in Longview, Texas. *The Case of the Russian Doll* is her first novel.

ABOUT THE AUTHOR

Lynn Nxabod attained an Art Lie. major in English Literature from Penn State University, then received a Juris Doctorate from the University of Pittsburgh School of Law. While a law school, she attended the Detention Center in Miami and joined Hutlington, where she worked. She passed the Bar in Pennsylvania and Nevada and practiced immigration law and housing law in Las Vegas. Her passion for the law has been to help refugees and low-income clients in illegal service companies and has received help. She had her first child, then decided to be a stay-at-home mom, and now loves spending time with her husband and three children in Longview, Texas. The Cost of Innocence is Nxabod's first novel.